The Feather Chase

A Crime~Solving Cousins Mystery

Shannon L. Brown

Sienna Bay Press

Cover Illustration and Lettering © 2014 Jeanine Henderson

ISBN: 978-0-9898438-0-5
Library of Congress Control Number: 2013917470

First Edition
Printed in the U.S.A.

To the special people in
my life past and present,
Thank you for always
believing in me

&

For everyone with
a dream

1

Maybe a Mystery

"We've been going uphill for ages. This was a dumb idea." Jessica stumbled on the uneven dirt path. Her cousin Sophie had brought her to the middle of nowhere to torment her.

"It wouldn't be dumb if you'd worn sneakers instead of those fancy sandals." Sophie glared at Jessica's feet. Looking up, she pointed to the right. "Check out Pine Lake. The water's sparkling in the sun."

Jessica glanced in that direction, then sat down on a boulder. What good was a lake in the distance? She tucked her hair behind her ears, pulled a bottle of fingernail polish out of her purse, and started painting her thumbnail her favorite shade of pink.

Out of the corner of her eye, she saw Sophie lower her arm. "I'm not going to let you make me miserable. Follow me—or stay here with the wild animals."

Wild animals? Jessica's gaze darted around the thick pine trees surrounding her. Then she leaped to her feet, knocking the open bottle onto a rock.

Sophie stood with her hands on her hips and looked at her with disgust. "Pick it up, or the woodsy police will give you a ticket."

Jessica grabbed it, then tried to wipe off the dirt that had stuck to the oozing fingernail polish, but there was no saving the bottle. She held it up in the air. "It's all your fault."

"My fault? I didn't ask for you to spend the summer at my house. You staying with us while your mom and dad are gone was our mothers' idea. We haven't seen each other since we were little kids, but they thought you should stay at my house for the summer?"

"I know." Jessica stared at the bottle in her hand and felt tears welling up in her eyes. She *wouldn't* cry in front of Sophie.

"Here." Sophie pulled a plastic bag out of her pocket and handed it to her. "This is left over from a snack the other day. Put the bottle in it. There's a trash can at the end of the trail."

Jessica carefully dropped the sticky bottle and brush into the bag and put it in her shorts pocket.

"Flip that rock over too. Pink nail polish doesn't belong in a forest." Sophie glared at her partially painted fingernails.

When Sophie continued up the hill, Jessica walked beside her but kept her eyes open for those wild animals. When a bush rubbed against her legs and a small leaf stuck to her shorts, she quickly brushed it off. "Can you tell me what the purpose of this walk is?"

"Didn't you think the lake was beautiful? Isn't it great just being in this forest?"

Jessica looked around and yawned, covering her mouth with her hand. "I don't like forests. I like shopping. I prefer city things." For probably the tenth time today, she wondered why her parents had sent her to a town in a forest. She liked living in London, England. Her house there overlooked a nicely groomed park. She didn't have to walk around in all this nature.

"Maybe the outdoors will grow on you. Pretend we're on a great adventure."

"I think twelve's a little too old for that."

"I'm twelve too, and I don't think so. My dad says you're never too old to use your imagination."

"Okay. We're on a great adventure." Jessica lowered her voice to a whisper. "We're going to find a bunch of spies around that bend in the path."

Sophie seemed startled, then grinned. She must not have known Jessica had a sense of humor.

As they rounded the next bend, Jessica pointed to the ground. "Look. There's a briefcase."

Sophie giggled. "You're really getting into this."

"No, I mean there *really* is a briefcase."

Sophie looked in the direction Jessica pointed. "There is!"

A black leather briefcase, something like her dad used to carry papers to meetings, lay on its side, next to a big pine tree. Jessica knelt beside it.

"No!" Sophie shouted when her cousin reached for it. "Don't you watch all those spy movies? The briefcase is booby-trapped."

"You must be kidding." Jessica poked at it with her finger. Then she picked it up off the ground. "Gee. Nothing happened." Setting it on a boulder, she pushed on the latches. "It's locked up tight."

"We'd better take it to the sheriff's office."

"Good idea. Maybe they'll give us a reward for bringing it to them."

"Don't count on it. It's *more* likely that my mom will let us have something sweet for dessert."

Jessica laughed. "What is it with your mom and sweets? Last night's dessert was a bowl of apples, so I had to cut mine up to eat it with these." She tapped a finger on her braces.

"She's sure sugar will kill us all. I hadn't thought about your braces. Let Mom know, and she'll get other kinds of fruit." Sophie bent over their discovery. "Now, let's see this thing. Seems like an ordinary briefcase to me."

"How many briefcases have you seen?"

Sophie stood. "Lots."

Jessica stared at her in disbelief.

"Well, lots on TV."

Jessica rolled her eyes.

Sophie walked around the area, checking under bushes and pushing aside pine branches.

"What are you doing?"

"I'm making sure nothing else is hiding here."

"It's just bushes and bugs." An insect flew around her a couple of times.

Sophie stopped and pursed her lips in an annoyed way. "There might be a tent or sleeping bag. This could be from a camper."

"You think someone went camping and took along something people carry to a business meeting?"

Sophie circled a tree. "People do strange things."

Yes, like this.

Sophie stood and brushed her hands off on her jeans. "Let's get this to the sheriff so we can see what's inside." She grabbed the briefcase and started walking down the trail. "I'm glad we're getting out of here long before it's dark. I don't want to have to wonder about whatever bad guy dropped this thing when owls are hooting and bats are flying."

Jessica glanced around the forest nervously. "Owls and bats? If they're out at night, where are they during the day?"

"They must be asleep."

Jessica stared up at the treetops. "What if someone wakes them up—by accident?"

"I don't think that can happen." Sophie checked her watch. "This is taking longer than I want it to. Follow me." She took off running down the path they'd come on, veering to the right, then down a steep, narrower path.

Jessica ran as fast as she could in her sandals. Her feet started to hurt, and the pain inched its way up her legs until they turned to Jell-O. Gasping for breath, she made a mental note to use her mom's exercise equipment when she got home and kept her focus on Sophie. Her sandal strap caught on a root in the path, but she jerked it free and stayed on her feet. A tiny image of long, brown hair in a ponytail, faded blue jeans, and a white T-shirt leaped over a small stream. Sophie hit the ground on the other side with both feet and kept running.

"Wait," Jessica yelled as loud as she could.

Sophie ground in her heels and came to a full stop as Jessica hurtled down the hill toward her, her arms flailing at her sides. As she got closer, Jessica decided not to jump the stream—she knew she couldn't make it—so she held her arms straight out and stepped from one rock to another.

About halfway across, Jessica asked, "Why didn't we come back over the bridge like when we left?"

"This way is faster. I usually run all the way home and jump over this stream in my backyard. I forgot about your sandals."

"They're fine where I'm from. We have sidewalks. There is no stream in my backyard. And you must admit the shoes look pretty good." She paused, thinking about which of two rocks to step on next. Only one more rock to go and she was over.

"I'm more of a sneaker kind of girl." Out of the corner of her eye, Jessica saw Sophie lift up her right foot. "See?"

"Can't look now." Jessica carefully stepped on the last rock she needed to cross the stream. When it shifted from side to side, she flapped her arms to keep her balance, then jumped to land. "Made it."

Sophie was standing in front of her with her eyes closed. She'd probably been waiting for a splash. She opened one eye slowly before opening the other. Yep, she had. "Let's get this to the sheriff." Sophie held up the briefcase.

"Slowly this time."

Sophie shrugged and said, "If we're going to walk slowly, let's at least take the shortcut through the woods into town."

"No problem."

They walked past Sophie's big white house, then through the woods. Jessica asked, "Do you know your sheriff?"

"Yeah, I've spent some time in the sheriff's office."

Jessica stopped. "Were you arrested?"

Sophie stopped beside her. "No. When I think I've found a mystery, I drop in and talk to her about it. Besides, her office is the most exciting place in town." She took a step and waved her on.

Jessica stepped beside her. "The sheriff's a woman?"

"Yep."

She thought about the hard-as-nails sheriffs and police officers she'd seen on TV and in the movies. "Is she tough—like a human bulldog?"

"Of course not," Sophie replied. "She's normal." She seemed to be thinking about her for a moment. "Sheriff Valeska is tall and has brown hair, but you usually can't see it because she has a sheriff's hat on top of it." Sophie turned to Jessica and looked her over. "I don't think she wears makeup or fingernail polish."

Jessica grimaced. She wouldn't leave the house without perfect makeup and hair.

"Sheriff Valeska is really nice, but she says my love of mysteries tries her patience sometimes." Sophie grinned.

Jessica laughed. Then she pictured her cousin's description of the sheriff and grimaced again.

When they got to town, they walked several blocks, past businesses and houses. Then Sophie led her through the door of the sheriff's office. It surprised her when they walked inside that a pretty woman in a uniform sat at a desk, and Sophie said, "Hi, Sheriff."

"Hi, Sophie." The sheriff smiled.

"Sheriff Valeska, this is my cousin Jessica Ballow."

"Pleased to meet you, Jessica. Sophie's mom told me you were arriving yesterday." Glancing from one to the other, she said, "Other than being about the same height, you're strikingly different."

Standing still while someone scrutinized her wasn't easy, but Jessica did her best to be polite. "Our moms are almost identical, but Sophie has her dad's brown hair and brown eyes, and I have my mom's blonde hair and green eyes."

"I think you'll enjoy your summer in Pine Hill, Jessica." The sheriff pushed back from her desk and smiled broadly. "Now, Sophie, I know from experience that you came here with a mystery. What's up?"

Sophie set the briefcase on the sheriff's desk and sat down on one of the avocado green plastic chairs in front of it. Jessica stayed out of the way and stood off to the side. After describing where they'd found the briefcase, Sophie asked, "So, do you think it belongs to a spy?"

Sheriff Valeska laughed. "I doubt that." She picked up the briefcase and examined it. "The bus stops at McGuire's Motel just outside of town. Nellie McGuire rarely remembers to turn on her No Vacancy sign when the motel's full. My guess is that someone got off the bus thinking they could get a room there but couldn't. The sign for Cutoff Trail is across the street from the motel, so they took it, hoping it was a shortcut to Pine Hill and another hotel. But it's a steep hill—"

"No kidding." Jessica sighed. "When we ran home, I was so out of breath I didn't think I'd ever catch up with Sophie."

"You aren't the first person who's gotten tired on one of Sophie's treks through the woods."

Jessica relaxed. Maybe she didn't need to work out.

"Go on, Sheriff," Sophie begged.

"Oh yes. The briefcase owner probably got tired when he or she neared the top of the hill and set down their luggage." Leaning back in her chair, she added, "My guess is that there's a suitcase near the place you found this briefcase."

Sophie's brown eyes sparkled. "Ooh, we'll have to search again."

The sheriff shook her head and grinned.

Sophie scooted to the front of the seat. "Come on, Sheriff, Let's see what's inside."

"Please open it!" Jessica urged the sheriff.

Jessica watched her push on the latches, then push again. When they didn't budge, the sheriff reached for the phone. "Homer, this is Mandy Valeska. I've got a locked briefcase here that needs to be opened. Okay. Sure." She hung up the phone.

"Is he coming now?" Sophie leaned forward in her chair, nearly tipping it over.

"No."

"What?" both girls said at the same time.

"He's got a woman up at the resort that accidentally locked her baby in the car. He'll be here in about a half hour. I need you two to be very quiet while you wait. I have a lot of work to do." She faced her computer and started typing.

Jessica sat in the chair next to Sophie, tapping her fingers on the arm of the chair until the sheriff stopped typing and frowned. She tucked her hand into her pocket and glanced around the room, her gaze coming back to the big clock on the wall every few minutes. A half hour with nothing to do was a very long time.

Finally, when she didn't think she could sit still a minute longer, a small man wearing worn jeans, a red flannel shirt, and wire-rimmed glasses that sat on the end of his nose entered the sheriff's office.

"Mr. Winston!" Sophie called out and turned toward Jessica. "He's our locksmith, so now we get to see what's in the briefcase. This is it."

Sheriff Valeska moved the briefcase to a table in the middle of the room. "Here you go, Homer."

He set a small leather satchel on the table, then picked up the briefcase and turned it from side to side, carefully examining the two locks. Then he reached into the satchel and took out a tool. "This will only," Mr. Winston said as he put it into one of the locks, "take a minute."

Jessica heard a small click.

He repeated the process on the other lock.

"There you go."

He put his tool back in his open bag, closed it, then picked up the bag and practically ran to the door.

"Thanks for coming, Homer," the sheriff called after him, "but don't you want to see what's in the briefcase?"

"No time." He gave a quick smile and waved as he went out the door. "Got to get over to Simpson's Shoes . . ." His voice faded away as the door closed behind him.

Sheriff Valeska turned toward Jessica and Sophie. "Are you girls ready for the big reveal?"

They crowded next to the sheriff as she popped the briefcase open.

2

Flying Fluff

Poof! White things flew into the air.

Sophie grabbed a handful, then opened her hand to see what they were. "It's raining feathers." Opening the briefcase was better than she'd imagined.

"Catch them, girls. We need to get these back in the briefcase." Sheriff Valeska rushed into a back room and returned with a white trash bag.

The three of them grabbed feathers out of the air and dropped them into the bag. When a deputy walked in the door, he stopped and stared wide-eyed at them until the sheriff said, "Hank, help us clean this up." Moving into action, he picked feathers up off the floor, adding them to the plastic bag.

A few minutes later, Jessica looked up and around. "There aren't any more feathers floating in the air."

The sheriff said, "I'll clear them off this table and we'll be done."

Sophie turned toward Jessica and giggled. "No, we won't. Jessica's covered. She must have been right in front of the briefcase when it opened." Sophie started plucking the feathers off her, then paused and studied a handful of them.

"Hurry up." Jessica shifted from one foot to the other.

Sophie turned the feathers over in her hand. "You know, there are little bits of white, fluffy stuff mixed in with the feathers."

Jessica lifted a feather off her wrist and dropped it in Sophie's hand.

"Okay, I get the message." Sophie dropped them in the bag, then walked around Jessica, looking her over. "She's clean."

Sophie peered into the open briefcase, then picked up two feathers that had stuck to the side and dropped them in the bag. "All the feathers are in the bag now."

Sheriff Valeska scowled. As she put a tie around the top of the plastic bag, she said, "But you added another set of fingerprints to the inside of the briefcase. Yours." She shook her head. "While there isn't anything illegal about feathers, I can't think of any reason someone would carry them around in a briefcase. I'm going to have a deputy dust this for fingerprints. And I'll have to get your fingerprints, Sophie, so he'll know to ignore them."

"My fingerprints!" Sophie said excitedly.

The sheriff laughed. "Someone else might be annoyed at having their fingerprints taken, but Sophie's excited."

"I'm learning that she's one of a kind," Jessica said.

Sheriff Valeska got out the fingerprinting materials, took all ten fingerprints, then pulled out a wipe and handed it to Sophie.

Sophie stared first at the wipe then at the black ink on her fingertips. Having the ink on her fingers might be fun. Then she could show people and tell them what had happened.

Jessica rolled her eyes. "Wipe it off, Sophie. It *won't* be fun to walk around with ink on your fingers."

Yeah, it probably would have been. Sophie gave in and took the wipe. "Other than when we first opened the briefcase and, of course, when I got fingerprinted, this wasn't as exciting as I'd hoped."

"Nope," Jessica said. "Not much excitement here. A pillow fight would have given us feathers—and fun."

"I'm not sure I agree." As Sheriff Valeska walked toward the back room with the briefcase and bag of feathers, she said, "I don't want to get you girls going again, but it's a bigger mystery than *I* expected. A briefcase full of feathers?" She vanished out of sight through a doorway.

"Now what?" asked Jessica.

Something at the edge of Sophie's vision caught her attention. She squinted and peered out of the corner of her eye. Almost cross-eyed, she reached up and plucked a feather out of her hair. "I guess all the feathers didn't land on you." Sophie held it up. The sheriff thought they had a mystery. Solving it would be much easier with their own feather. "This can be our first clue."

"Actually, it's Sheriff Valeska's clue. It's now property of the sheriff's office."

"Sheriff?" Sophie called out.

"Yes, Sophie?" the sheriff answered from the storeroom.

"Can we borrow the feather I just found in my hair?"

After what seemed like a long pause, she said, "Well, since you found the briefcase and there are so many feathers, go ahead. But remember you're just borrowing it and have to bring it back."

"Gotcha." Sophie rushed over and opened the door with one hand, clutching the feather in the other. She said to Jessica in a low voice, "Let's get out of here before she changes her mind."

"Absolutely."

Once out the door, Sophie went straight to a bench on the sidewalk and motioned for Jessica to sit next to her. When Jessica was seated, Sophie covered her mouth with her hand and said, "See that man?"

Jessica leaned closer. "I can barely hear you."

"I said, 'See that man?'" Sophie replied in a slightly louder voice and gestured to the right with her thumb.

Jessica started to turn that way.

"No! Be subtle. Don't let him know you're watching him."

Jessica hummed softly, and with an almost believable casual look, turned that direction. "I see a man in a brown suit and a rust-colored tie."

"That's him."

"That's who?"

"That's the man who stole the money from the bank and left it in the briefcase in the woods."

"You've lost it. By the way, I thought the briefcase belonged to a spy."

"Spy, bank robber, it could be either one."

"And don't you always have strangers in this town?"

"Well . . . there are always tourists at the resort—but look at that guy."

"I can't."

"Why?"

"He's gone."

Sophie whipped around. "He was wearing a suit. Almost no one wears a suit in Pine Hill. Even the tourists. They dress in brand-new, relaxed-type clothes. Sometimes I think I could find a price tag hanging off them if I got close."

Jessica giggled. "They can't be that bad."

"The clothes are. But the people are usually okay. They just want to relax. As the ads say, 'Come to Pine Hill in the mountains to unwind. Let clean air and sparkling water revive you.'"

"You're kidding."

"Nope. Men leave their suits behind. From what I can tell, it's tough to relax in a suit and tie." Sophie pulled her shirt tightly around her neck like she was wearing a tie. Her breathing cut off and she let it go, gasping for air. "Whew. I can see why."

Jessica settled down next to her on the bench. "Let's work out a plan of action."

"Agreed. First we need to find out all we can about this feather."

"Good plan. Let's get on your computer and Google 'feathers.'" Jessica started to stand.

Sophie grabbed her arm and pulled her back down. "It isn't that easy."

"Huh?"

"I'm surprised you haven't asked about a computer before. Or cell phone access."

"Mom said she'd text me when she arrived in the Middle East where Dad's working, and I knew that wouldn't be until later today. I'd just assumed you hadn't needed to text or call anyone on your phone."

"I don't have a cell phone. It wouldn't matter much if I did anyway. The reception in town is okay but not great, and almost zero outside of town."

Jessica pulled her phone out of her bag. "Nothing."

"Told you. You might have service a block away. They say it's because of the mountains."

Jessica tucked her phone back into her purse. "Well, it's easier to use a computer with a larger screen for something like this anyway."

"Um . . ." Sophie looked down. This felt more than a little embarrassing.

"Is your computer broken?"

"That's just it. Mom likes things that are old, and doesn't like things that are new. She also thinks I'd find a way to get in trouble on the Internet."

Jessica sprang to her feet. "You don't mean—"

Sophie sighed. "Yep. We don't have a computer. Well, other than the one Dad has in his office since he works at home, but that's only for his business."

"How do you do projects for school?"

"I go to the library."

"Great. I like libraries." Jessica sounded kind of nervous when she quickly said, "Is it a brick building like all of these?"

Sophie nodded, then stood. "We do seem to like brick here. The library's only a few blocks from here. I go there a lot."

On the way there, Jessica stopped in front of a drugstore. "Let's run in here, Sophie. I want to replace the fingernail polish I dropped."

"Sure." Sophie followed Jessica through the cosmetics section to an area with dozens of bottles of nail polish. "So many colors."

"The choice isn't just about color. There's frosted or not, and other things, too." Jessica scanned the shelves, searching through lots of polish. "I found it! It's the perfect pink." She held up a bottle of nail polish.

Sophie shrugged. One pink looked pretty much like another.

"It's the same as the one that got ruined. It was my favorite." She clutched it to her chest and rushed to the cash register.

When they were standing in line, Sophie felt like a jerk. "Um, I think that was my fault." She tapped the top of the bottle in Jessica's hand. "You know, that it fell. I think I should pay for it."

"How 'bout we split the cost? It was stupid of me to be doing my nails in the middle of a hike."

Sophie pulled money out of her back pocket, gave it to her, and Jessica took the rest out of her purse.

Stepping into the library made Jessica feel at home for the first time since she'd arrived in Pine Hill. She had to play it cool, though, because if Sophie knew she spent a lot of time in libraries, her cousin might figure out that she was the extra-smart type. Then she might not fit in here, just like she didn't seem to fit in anywhere else.

Sophie typed "birds" in the online catalog. A long list of books flashed onto the screen. "Wow. Twenty-two books. Something in here should solve the mystery."

Jessica peered over Sophie's shoulder and laughed. "The first two are books for little kids, and the third one is a turkey cookbook."

Sophie paged through the list. "Here's one that sounds good. *Birds of North America.* And here's another one that might help. *Raising Ducks and Geese for Fun and Profit.* Maybe the feather is from a duck or a goose." She checked through the rest of the list and sighed. "Only two useful books out of twenty-two."

After writing down the two call numbers, she tore the paper in half. "I'll find this one and you find the other one," she said as she handed Jessica the bottom half of the paper. "Let's meet"—she looked around the room, then pointed at a couple of chairs—"there."

Jessica loved wandering through the stacks, seeing what this library had to offer. It took her longer than she'd expected to return with the book she'd been assigned. Sophie was already flipping through her book, so Jessica sat and started checking hers out.

A minute later, Sophie sighed as she closed the book and set it on the table next to her chair. "Is yours useless, too?"

"It's only helpful if you want to buy a few ducks or geese and stick them in your backyard."

Sophie grinned. "Interesting thought, but I don't think Mom and Dad would go for it. Mine showed pictures of birds, but no up-close feather photos.

"We'll have to find another way to get answers." Placing her hand on her stomach, Jessica said, "I'm starving. Do you know when we're having dinner?"

"Mom can't leave her antique shop until the last customer leaves. Then she comes home to cook dinner. Dad *isn't* good in the kitchen." Sophie shuddered.

"Let's hurry to your house. Maybe the customers left early."

Sophie patted her pocket. "I'll be happy to have the feather in a safe place at home."

As they walked, Jessica thought about the briefcase full of feathers. They could just leave the whole thing to the sheriff, but Jessica already knew Sophie well enough to be sure she wouldn't like that idea. She figured Sophie must be thinking about the feathers too, because she hadn't seen her stay quiet this long.

When they turned onto the shortcut through the woods to Sophie's house, her cousin finally broke her silence. "We should be working on our mystery."

"Cousin, we just *found* a briefcase. I admit that having feathers inside it is strange, but we don't know for sure that there is a mystery."

"The sheriff said it was a mystery. I think bad guys chased a criminal through the woods, and the criminal dropped the briefcase."

"And the guy chasing him didn't notice when he tripped over it?" Jessica shook her head.

"It was off to the side of the trail, so he wouldn't have tripped. Anyway, think about the mystery."

Trying to appear very serious, Jessica said, "I'll give it my deepest thought."

Sophie rolled her eyes. "Why don't I believe you? The big question is: why did someone leave the briefcase out in the open on the path, where anyone could see it, and why was it filled with feathers?"

"That's two questions."

"Whatever. Do you ever get that funny feeling that someone's watching you?" Sophie asked as she glanced around.

Jessica shrugged. "Sometimes. Why?"

"How about now?" Sophie stopped and glanced over her shoulder.

"Nothing." Jessica stared up into the tall trees, then around to the path behind them. "Everything seems normal, at least as normal as a forest ever seems to me."

"I keep getting the feeling that someone's watching." Sophie snapped her fingers. "I know. It's the guy in the brown suit."

Jessica studied the ground. Pushing a rock to the side with her foot, she studied it. Then she raked a pile of leaves aside.

"What are you doing?"

"I'm looking for your mind. You must have lost it around here because you seemed intelligent just a short time ago."

"Funny. Let's be quiet and see if we hear anything."

A loud cracking sound made them both jump.

3

Hiding Secrets

Jessica whispered, "What was that?"

"A branch breaking."

The girls looked at each other and Sophie whispered, "It could be just an animal."

A chill went through Jessica. "You're telling me it's either a wild animal or a criminal?"

"That does sound bad." Sophie peered over her shoulder one last time, then whispered, "I'll beat you home."

"No, you won't," Jessica whispered back.

A second later, Sophie took off running, and Jessica chased after her. When the heel on Jessica's sandal caught on a tree root, she grabbed the tree's trunk and swung around it, barely stopping herself from falling. Her shoes seemed to catch on everything in her path. If running from spies and thieves was going to be part of her life in Pine Hill, she would, unfortunately, have to wear sneakers.

Sophie's big, old, white house came into view around a bend in the path. They ran up the steps, pulled open the wooden screen door, and skidded to a stop.

"We're home," Sophie called out.

Jessica's racing heart started to beat a little more normally when her aunt April answered from the kitchen, "Dinner in twenty, girls."

They fell onto the sofa, panting. Sophie set the feather on the coffee table and between breaths said, "Let's examine the evidence."

Jessica picked up the feather and studied it. "Remember the fluffy white things that were with the feathers?"

"Yes, but I don't know what they were."

"That's another piece of the puzzle that's missing."

"You know, it's complicated enough just finding out about this feather." Sophie tapped her chin with her finger. "We should ignore the fluffy stuff for now."

"Good idea. I've thought about feathers enough. Let's hide this and take a feather break."

"Agreed. For now." Sophie grabbed it out of Jessica's hand and walked into her bedroom.

Jessica followed her. "Where can we keep the feather that's safe?" Jessica glanced around the room. Under the lamp? No, it might blow out if someone opened the window. In the drawer in the nightstand? No, too obvious. Maybe . . . she noticed Sophie kneeling in her closet.

"What are you doing?" Jessica pushed clothes on hangers out of the way and knelt beside her. "Do you have some kind of secret hiding place?"

"The best." Sophie used a bent hanger to pry up one of the floorboards, then reached in and pulled a metal box the size of a big paperback book out of the hole.

"That's great! Did you make this hole?"

"No. The board's been loose all my life. But I was reading a book where a loose board in a closet hid a treasure."

"So you threw down the book and ran to the closet."

Sophie nodded her head. "You can't imagine how excited I was when I pried up the board, and inside I found a metal box."

"And?"

"And it was empty." She sighed. "Too bad, but it makes a great hiding place." Sophie dropped the feather in the box, fit it back in the hole, and replaced the board.

After dinner, Sophie, Jessica, and Sophie's dad, Lucas Sandoval, waited for Sophie's mom to bring the bowl of fruit, but she came through the kitchen door carrying a yellow box instead.

"Dessert?" Her mom hadn't given them an actual dessert in months.

"I knew you girls would be hungry after wandering around in the woods all morning, so I bought you a surprise at Bananas." When she set the open box on the table, they leaned over to peer inside.

"I see slices of cake and a plastic container with," Sophie picked it up, "strawberries in it. Wow! Strawberry shortcake." She set it down and licked her lips.

"Correction," Mrs. Sandoval said. "Strawberries on banana shortcake. You know how Abigail Bowman is about bananas."

Sophie laughed and turned to Jessica. "She puts them in everything in her bakery, but the weird thing is that it's all good. I guess you could say she's bananas about bananas."

Jessica groaned.

"She was trying out a chocolate chip cookie when I stopped in today."

"With bananas?" Jessica grimaced.

"No. She wanted to see if other people liked things without bananas."

They all laughed.

Mrs. Sandoval snapped her fingers. "I almost forgot. I bought some cream for you." She went back into the kitchen and returned with two cans of whipped cream. "I've got some paperwork to do, so I'll leave you guys to it."

Mr. Sandoval said, "Dessert is a special occasion for us. You need to visit more often, Jessica." He put strawberries on cake, covered it with whipped cream after reading the directions on the can, then put a spoonful of his dessert in his mouth. "Mmmm."

Jessica and Sophie made their shortcake. Then each grabbed a can of whipped cream. Sophie stopped to read the directions on the can.

As Jessica squirted hers, she said, "Uncle Lucas, you and Sophie act like you've never seen a can of whipped cream before."

"We haven't." He put the can down and took a bite of shortcake.

"What? Really?"

Sophie said, "Well, we've never seen a can of whipped cream in this house." Slowly eating a bite, she enjoyed the thrill of having dessert. "Yum."

"Now I understand why you had to read the directions and you have two cans for three people. You've got enough here for you and your closest friends."

Mr. Sandoval laughed. "None of us knew we had too much. Oh, this is so good."

Jessica tasted hers. "It is. And the banana shortcake is delicious." She wiped off some cream that splashed on the table, then asked, "This table is big and heavy. It seems old, so I wondered, is it an antique?"

"Almost everything in our house is an antique. Mom loves them, and she doesn't like much that's new." As Sophie took another bite, her mind shifted to the mystery, and she pictured a man running with a briefcase through the woods. "You know, Jessica, I like my theory about spies in Pine Hill."

Mr. Sandoval made choking sounds.

Sophie ran into the kitchen, coming back with a glass of water. Her dad took a sip. "Spies?" he croaked, then took a long drink of water.

"Sure, Dad." Sophie explained what had happened that day.

He sat back and laughed. "I know I've told you over and over to use your imagination, but you might be overdoing it, Soph."

"You wait and see." Sophie knew they'd stumbled upon something exciting. She knew a mystery was waiting to be solved.

4

A Creamy Mess

Jessica stretched and watched the pattern of morning sunlight on the wall as it filtered through the trees outside her window. Morning. Worse yet, morning a long way from home. She'd spent every other summer with her mother and brother somewhere in Europe, her dad joining them when he could get away from work. Except for when they'd all gone to Thailand the summer Dad worked there.

Rolling over, she squinted at her cousin.

"Good morning," Sophie said, radiating happiness.

Jessica grunted. Mornings were, well ... early in the day. And there wasn't a reason to be happy.

Sophie added, "Isn't this a beautiful day?"

Jessica squinted again, then blinked a few times.

"See the sunshine coming through the window?"

Jessica blinked then grunted again. No matter how hard she'd tried in the past, she'd never been able to make complete sentences first thing in the morning.

Sophie rolled over, turning her back to her. "Maybe you should just get out of here and go take your shower."

Jessica stared at Sophie's back, wishing her parents were here. They'd sent her to this strange place where she didn't know anyone. And now her cousin was being mean to her again. Jessica got up, grabbed her robe off the end of the bed, and trudged into the bathroom.

"Hurry up," Sophie shouted. "You don't need six pounds of makeup here."

Jessica bit her tongue to hold back the tears. That horrible person wasn't going to make her cry. She hurried into the shower, feeling better the longer she was awake.

After her shower, Jessica opened the drawer in Sophie's dresser that she'd been given along with half the closet. She chose hot pink shorts with flowers on them and a matching pink T-shirt. Then she dried her hair, deciding to leave it straight, only touching it up with a flat iron. Blush, lip gloss, and mascara—and a quick repair of her less-than-perfect fingernail polish—completed her look.

She wandered around the house for a few minutes. Hearing noises, she pushed open the kitchen door. Sophie, Miss Sunshine, stood at the counter, wearing an old white T-shirt and the usual faded jeans. Jessica didn't think she'd bought the jeans faded either because they looked like they'd been around a long time. Instead of fixing her hair differently today, she'd pulled it into another ponytail.

"I'm having strawberry shortcake for breakfast." Sophie glared at her in a way that said, *Do you have a problem with that?*

"Sounds great." Jessica smiled, trying to be cheerful as she put some of the leftover cake in a bowl and spooned strawberries over it. But Sophie continued being nasty.

"Here." Sophie slammed a can of whipped cream in front of her, then got the other one out of the fridge. When she squirted the cream in her bowl, it splattered onto Jessica's arm.

Jessica stared at her arm. She just knew Sophie had done that on purpose. Pointing her can at her cousin, she pushed the top. Whipped cream flew onto Sophie's chin and splashed her hair.

Sophie blinked, then reached up and touched her chin.

Uh-oh, Jessica thought, *I definitely should not have done that.*

Sophie pointed her can at her and squirted it. Jessica could feel the whipped cream covering her hair.

She pushed on her can's nozzle and sprayed Sophie with all her might, covering her from head to toe. Her cousin just stood there, stunned. Finally, when Jessica's can sputtered, spit, and stopped, Sophie turned on her, letting her cream fly. Jessica put up her hands to block the flow, but she could feel the gloppy cream hitting her head, her feet, and everything in between.

When that can made sputtering sounds, Sophie glanced down at it, then around the kitchen. "Oh, no!"

Jessica followed her gaze. Whipped cream had splashed onto the cupboards, countertops, and fridge. "We're in trouble now."

"Maybe not. If we can get this cleaned up before Mom or Dad sees it . . ."

Jessica grabbed the dishrag and started wiping the front of a cupboard. "Do you think the whipped cream will hurt the wood the cupboards and floor are made of?"

"No. They're even older than Mom and Dad. They've seen it all." Sophie pulled out a mop, got it wet, and wiped the floor.

A short time later, Sophie leaned the mop against the counter, then slowly turned in a full circle. "Whew. I think that's it."

Jessica threw her rag in the sink. "Finally. When I wiped off the full coffeepot, I realized your dad might come in to get some before we finished. But we made it."

Now that they had the kitchen clean, Jessica really looked at Sophie for the first time. She was leaning against the cupboards and covered in whipped cream from her hair to her knees. Jessica giggled. When Sophie seemed puzzled, she pointed at her.

Sophie looked down at herself, then at Jessica. For a few seconds Jessica thought she would yell at her, but instead she burst out laughing.

That made Jessica start laughing. She laughed so hard that she crumpled to the ground, holding her aching middle.

Sophie slowly slid down the cupboards and landed on the floor beside her. "I didn't know you knew how to laugh," she gasped between words.

"You were so mean that I thought you never laughed."

"I wasn't mean. You were. You were nice after we found the briefcase, so I thought you were a nice person."

Jessica stopped laughing. "Me mean? What about this morning? You yelled at me about my makeup."

Sophie wrinkled her brow. "That's because you were nasty right away. You got out of bed and didn't say a word."

"I never talk in the morning."

"Never?"

"Never. Mom says I'm the worst person in the morning that she's ever seen or heard of."

Sophie stared at her in disbelief. "I didn't notice it yesterday morning."

"I'd traveled the day before, so I slept in. You were already up and didn't see me until after my shower."

"I'll remember not to talk to you when you first wake up. Your photo is next to the word grumpy in the dictionary." Sophie leaned over and hugged her. "I'm sorry, Jessica."

Jessica hugged her back. "Me too."

The kitchen door swung open, and Sophie's dad walked in carrying a mug. Jessica held her breath, hoping he'd be thinking about something else, get his coffee, and not notice his cream-covered daughter and niece on the floor. Instead, he poured a cup of coffee, then reached down to swipe his finger through the whipped cream on Sophie's cheek before turning and walking toward the door, licking it off. "Soph, you'd better replace the whipped cream before your mom knows it's gone."

Jessica watched him walk out the door. "He didn't yell," she said in amazement.

"I knew I had a great dad, but he's even greater than I thought." Sophie looked at the empty cans of whipped cream on the counter. "But he's right. Mom sees food as something that's not to be played with." Sophie stood. "Let's finish with this mess, then wash our clothes and us. We can go to the grocery store for whipped cream this afternoon—after we've done some sleuthing." She had that excited *I love a mystery expression* again.

5

Shoes and Clues

Jessica dreaded the next thing she needed to do. "Before we leave, I have to get something."

"Huh?"

Jessica held up her right foot. "Shoes."

"You'll have to excuse me for saying this, but you have a lot of shoes."

"Yes," Jessica said, "but not shoes I can run in."

"Now you're talking. Let's go get some at Simpson's Shoes."

"Not necessary." Jessica furrowed her brow as she thought. "But why does that name sound familiar?"

"Mr. Winston was on his way there after he opened the briefcase."

"Ah, yes. No, I just need my suitcase." She just didn't see any other choice.

"You said 'shoes' and now you want your suitcase? Are you leaving?"

Where would she go? "No. I didn't unpack everything."

Sophie waved her on.

They went outside and through the side door of a separate garage, where Sophie pointed to a suitcase leaning against the back wall. Jessica exhaled deeply and opened it. Then she reached into the side pocket.

Sophie bent over her. "Do you have shoes in there?"

As Jessica pulled out first one shoe and then the other, Sophie exclaimed, "Sneakers! You have sneakers, but you've been hiking in sandals?"

"Mom made me pack them. I've only worn them in gym class and didn't want them this summer."

"Your mom's smart."

Jessica held up the white, slightly worn shoes. She sighed. "I guess so." After slipping them on, she walked around the room. They would work. But they weren't cute.

"You seem sad, cousin. How 'bout if I treat you to lunch at Donadio's Deli?"

"I am hungry." Jessica tried hard to smile. "At least I can run now. Of course, I hope I don't *need* to run."

When they got to town, Jessica read the signs as they walked by stores. Walking past the window of the shoe store the locksmith had mentioned, she said, "Ooh, love those blue flats. We'll have to come back here." Still reading store signs, she ran into Sophie's back. *Whap.*

Sophie caught her before she fell. "We're here." She pushed Jessica upright and held open the glass door.

When Jessica looked up, a dark-haired boy behind the deli counter was staring at them and laughing. "You didn't tell me a cute boy worked here. And he saw clumsy me run into you," she whispered to her cousin as they walked inside.

"Who?" Sophie followed Jessica's gaze. "Oh, you mean Tony. His parents own this place."

Tony made their sandwiches. Jessica had a veggie on whole wheat with chips, Sophie had roast beef on white with potato salad. He didn't say much but seemed to be nice. And oh, so cute.

When they sat down, Sophie whispered to her, "You think Tony's cute?"

"Yeesss." Jessica took a bite of her sandwich. He'd put on just the right amount of mustard.

Sophie shrugged. "I never thought much about him. He sometimes hangs out with me and my friend Megan." She started eating her sandwich. "He's really brainy."

Jessica's heart started beating faster. Maybe if she hung out with smart people this summer, she would get used to it. Then she might be able to relax and be herself when she got home. "What subjects is he good at?"

"Science and math. I think." Just then, several more customers walked in the door. "But he's probably going to be too busy here this summer to even learn your name."

Jessica sighed. "It doesn't matter, because we have to solve this mystery. Besides, he may not like girls with braces." Jessica clamped her mouth shut over the braces she'd gotten last March—the braces she tried to pretend weren't there and weren't reflecting light that blinded everyone in the room. Her mom would tell her that no one noticed them, that she was exaggerating. She knew better.

"I've known Tony for a long time, and I doubt he cares if you have braces." Sophie finished her sandwich, then sat back with her soda in her hand.

Jessica popped a chip in her mouth, crunched it, then started coughing when Tony spoke from behind her. Taking a big drink of her soda, she looked up at him.

"Hi, Sophie. Having a good summer?"

"Good so far. This is my cousin, Jessica."

"I heard you were visiting."

Jessica's face went hot, but she hoped not red, when Tony smiled at her.

Turning to Sophie, he asked, "Did you hear that someone unlocked the doors at Simpson's Shoes during the night?"

Sophie wrinkled her brow. "Just unlocked? They didn't steal anything?"

"That's what my dad said." He shrugged. "They're open today, so they couldn't have taken much. Heard from Megan?"

"I got a postcard from her." Sophie grinned at him. "She commented on the cute guys in Florida."

He burst out laughing. "Sounds like Megan." A group walked in the door, and he started for the counter, saying over his shoulder, "Back to work."

After he left, Jessica asked, "I haven't met Megan, right?"

"Nope. Her family is spending the summer at a beach near her grandmother's house."

"Ah. I wondered why you didn't have any friends." As soon as she'd said it, Jessica cringed, wondering if she'd offended her cousin.

Sophie laughed and poked Jessica in the arm. "I have friends. But they're either helping at a family business or out of town." She grabbed a chip off Jessica's plate. "We do need to find out more about the feather. That should lead us to why someone filled a briefcase with them."

Jessica looked down at the remaining bite of her sandwich. "This is so good."

"Everything here is great." Sophie stared off into space. "I wonder if the unlocked doors at Simpson's Shoes are a clue."

"A shoe store has nothing in common with feathers."

"You're right about the lack of a connection with a shoe store. But mysteries can be mysterious."

Jessica rolled her eyes. "I can't believe you said that."

6

Danger Run

Outside the deli, Sophie started to turn right, then stopped. She had a better idea. "How about a milkshake?"

"Seriously?" Jessica said. "After what we just ate?"

"The resort—the big building up the hill—makes the best shakes. They also have a big display of wildlife from this area in the lobby. Maybe they'll have info about our feather." They started in that direction. "Besides, I've got room for a shake."

"I'm surprised, but so do I. It must be all this exercise."

As they climbed the hill, Sophie checked out the sky in all directions. "It's getting gray and cloudy. But I don't think it looks like rain."

"I hope not. It wouldn't be fun getting caught in it this far from your house."

Sophie shrugged. They'd dry off if they did. Jessica might think it was a big deal though.

Toward the top of the hill, Jessica stopped. "Sophie, this place is like a mansion, and I'm just wearing shorts and a T-shirt. You're in jeans."

"We're fine. Remember, people come here to relax."

As they neared the building and a limousine pulled up to the door, Jessica nervously touched the front of her shirt and ran her fingers through her hair. When they walked in the door, she let out a giant sigh of relief. "It's really elegant in here. Chandeliers. Tables with white tablecloths. But everyone *is* dressed like us." Jessica nodded toward a group of men in suits. "Except for them."

"Suits, huh?"

"Maybe the guy in the suit is staying here with that group."

"That's possible." She wouldn't give up on any clue though. Not yet.

Jessica turned in a full circle. "This lobby is gorgeous. There's even a huge waterfall so it sounds like I'm outside, but I didn't have to run up the side of a mountain to see it."

Sophie laughed. "I'll have you loving the outdoors soon. Just as in mysteries, the waterfall isn't as simple as it seems. It has a secret."

Jessica eyed her suspiciously. "How can it have a secret?"

Sophie glanced around the room. No one seemed to be watching them. Around to the side of the falls, she opened a shorter-than-normal door. "This passage goes right through, but they don't tell visitors to the resort. Probably because you get really wet."

"Makeup running down my face and hair hanging wet doesn't sound good to me." Jessica stepped back.

"The display about birds is over here." Sophie motioned for Jessica to follow her across the room.

A glassed-in display had photos of the birds in Pine Hill. But no pictures of feathers. "I thought we'd get *something* from this."

Jessica pointed at a brass engraved plaque on the wall. "This says, 'State Fish and Game assistance on this display gratefully acknowledged.' Maybe they could help us."

"Fish and Game. Why didn't I think of that? We can call them first thing Monday." Sophie turned toward Jessica. "I feel like we got some help with the mystery. Ready for pure deliciousness?"

"Always."

They chose one of the small tables scattered throughout the lobby and ordered shakes, Jessica's chocolate and Sophie's filled with tropical fruit.

As soon as the server left, Jessica asked, "Did I really hear you order something with fruit?"

"Mom makes me eat it so much that I know I should hate it, but I love it."

"I like chocolate." Jessica licked her lips.

Sophie grimaced. "I'll work on the outdoors with you, and you can work on chocolate with me."

Jessica shook her head. "I think it will be easier for you to love chocolate than it will be for me to love the outdoors."

When their shakes came, Jessica did a happy dance in her chair. "Ooh, a chocolate milkshake that's topped with whipped cream, chocolate chips, and white chocolate shavings. Perfect for a chocolate connoisseur like myself."

Sophie stared at her. "There you go again. Sometimes you don't sound like a kid. Must come from living all over the world."

"Maybe." Jessica seemed almost guilty about something. She turned in her chair and looked around the lobby. "Sophie, there's a man in a brown suit over there." She gestured with her head toward the front door.

Sophie turned that direction. "There is. He's probably with the other men in suits."

"I don't think so. I can tell that his suit doesn't fit well. The other men are wearing suits that appear tailored to fit." Jessica smiled. "Spending time shopping pays off."

Suddenly, a man Sophie had never seen before pulled out a chair and sat down at their table. "I'm interested in the feathers you found."

"Feathers?" Sophie asked innocently. He was wearing a gray suit, not brown, so maybe the criminal, maybe not. A man could own more than one suit.

"I know about them." He reached into his suit coat pocket.

Before he could pull out a gun, Sophie grabbed Jessica by the hand and pulled her to her feet. They had to get out of here to protect themselves and all of the people around them.

"We're leaving. Don't follow us. There are a lot of people here watching you." She swept her hand through the air toward other tables. "If you don't want me to scream, don't try to come after us."

They backed away for a few feet. Then Sophie pulled Jessica along and they half walked, half ran through the lobby.

"What are you doing?" Jessica tried to skid to a stop, but Sophie tugged her forward.

Sophie said, "He must be the man who owns the briefcase. And he might have been pulling a gun out of his pocket."

"Maybe not. He might be with the police."

"Not a chance. I know all the deputies."

Jessica asked in a high-pitched voice, "What if we *are* being followed by a criminal?" She turned to see if he was there and stumbled, but Sophie kept her on her feet. "He's following us."

Sophie tore through the lobby toward the waterfall. "Here. He can't see us from where he is." Pulling open the door, she pushed Jessica through it and they huddled near the floor. Peering out one of the holes that let in light, she didn't see anyone suspicious. When she glanced over at Jessica, she found her cousin crouched next to her with a stupid expression on her face, staring at a blank wall.

Sophie nudged her. "Jessica?"

Jessica blinked and water ran down her face.

"You okay?"

Jessica nodded slowly. "Are we safe?"

Sophie checked the peephole again. "He's gone." She carefully surveyed the lobby from one side to the other. "I don't see the man in the brown suit either."

"I'm sorry I seemed to freeze, but considering the stress of the moment, it's understandable," Jessica said as she studied the room.

Sophie stared at her. "What?"

Jessica sounded nervous as she said, "I read something about it."

Sophie shook her head, spraying water everywhere like a wet dog. Then she stepped out of the door and started back toward their table, checking the other tables and the rest of the room to make sure the men had left. "I know we're a little wet, but it was the only place I could think of in a hurry."

Jessica wiped water off her arms. "I'd rather be wet and safe." She picked up her half-melted milkshake. "My hair's flat, my makeup must be a mess, and this doesn't look as good as it did before. You want to stay?"

"Actually, I've been thinking about how no one knows we're here, so let's go *after* I call home to check in."

They checked Jessica's phone—no bars—so Sophie used a hotel phone against the wall, and they put her call through.

When they reached the edge of town walking home, it started to sprinkle.

"Yikes. More water." Jessica swiped at her cheek and picked up speed. She could really move when she had to.

As they turned onto the driveway, big drops of rain plopped down. Darting up the driveway, they took the porch steps two at a time.

Inside, Jessica followed Sophie into her room. "I'm cold and wet." She shivered. "I'm going to put on a sweater and jeans."

Sophie whirled around. "You own jeans?"

"Of course." She pulled them and a sweater out of her dresser drawer, then changed her clothes and dropped her wet clothes over the side of the bathtub.

"Why haven't I seen your jeans before?"

"Because," she turned in the mirror to check out the outfit, nodding with approval, "I don't wear jeans very often."

"What about school?"

"Uniform."

Sometimes Sophie felt like her cousin lived on another planet. Then again, a uniform would make it easy to get dressed in the morning. "Since we hurried home, I think we have time to call Fish and Game before they close. Otherwise we have to wait all weekend." She left to find the number in a phone book, then came back. "Why don't you listen and remind me if I forget to tell them something."

Sophie told the person on the other end of the line what they needed, then hung up.

"That was too fast. What happened?" Jessica asked.

"The waterfowl biologist just left for a two-week vacation."

Jessica groaned. "Well, it was a good idea. I guess we won't be able to see the sheriff about the mystery any more until Monday, since her office will be closed. We have the weekend off."

"She's usually there on Saturdays."

Jessica sighed. "Only you would know that. Then let's not talk about the mystery anymore tonight."

Sophie started to argue, then realized that Jessica didn't love mysteries and they'd had quite a mysterious day. She picked up her book and sat down to read. Her cousin got a call from her parents, and she grinned from ear to ear the rest of the night.

When Sophie went to bed, she was glad to be in a safe place. Her eyes started to close; then she blinked. Were they really safe here, though? Was someone trying to get to them to find out about the feathers?

Sophie sat on the end of her cousin's bed, a few feet from where Jessica had set up her hair care and makeup products in front of her dresser mirror last night, what her cousin had called her "beauty station." Jessica had scowled as she'd walked to the shower, but Sophie thought she'd be okay by the time she started to dry her hair.

"Jessica, it's sunny outside," Sophie shouted over the hair dryer. "Let's walk to the sheriff's office and see if she's learned anything new about the feathers."

Jessica turned off the dryer and smoothed her hair in the mirror. "We could call and find that out."

Whew. She had timed it right. "I thought she might tell us more if we were in front of her."

Jessica picked up a tube of something and smeared it on her face. "You're probably right."

"Maybe she'll have something new to help us solve the mystery."

Putting in her earrings, Jessica said, "I'll keep getting ready while you talk. Makeup and mysteries go well together." She reached for the tube of what Sophie now knew was mascara.

When Jessica said she'd finished, her blonde hair was perfectly styled and her makeup was perfect for, well, shopping at the mall. She and her cousin didn't have much in common, but at least they had the mystery to work on together. "Let's go see the sheriff."

Jessica got dressed, and then they had a quick breakfast of cold cereal before leaving. Sophie closed the front door and shouted, "Race you."

Jessica, a few feet in front of her, took off running. She seemed to be moving faster now that she had her sneakers, but it only took a minute to pass her.

In front of the sheriff's office, they found a deputy directing traffic around a four-car accident, and the sheriff appeared to be interviewing the drivers.

Jessica cocked her head to the side. "Doesn't seem like anyone was hurt."

"Nope, and the cars only have little dents. I wonder why?"

Sheriff Valeska picked something up off the sidewalk, then walked up the nearby alley.

Jessica said, "I'm guessing that the sheriff will be a while longer. Maybe we should go inside and wait."

"Good idea."

As soon as they'd stepped inside, Sophie pointed and said, "Look!" then ran through the building and out the back door.

"Sophie!" Jessica hurried after her.

7

Clue Two

"Hey!" Sophie yelled at the man sprinting down the alley.

He held a brown jacket over the side of his head, making it impossible to see his face, and glanced over his shoulder.

"Stop!"

When he glanced back again, he stumbled, and white things dropped out of the jacket as he fell forward and caught himself with his arms. Then kneeling, he pushed and pulled on something before glancing back at her. Tugging sideways at it, he fell over, then shoved his hand into his pocket, climbed to his feet, and took off running again.

Sophie chased him down the alley to the street, where Jessica caught up with her. "Rats. He vanished."

"Who?"

"A man. He acted suspicious when he ran out of the sheriff's office."

"You're making a mystery again. Maybe he ran because a crazy girl shouting at him and chasing him made him really nervous."

"No. He had a brown jacket. It's him. Let's go see if he left some evidence in the alley."

They walked up and down the alley, but as far as Sophie could tell, nothing appeared suspicious. "He fell about here, behind either Kendall's Jewelers or Pine Hill Gifts." She studied the ground.

Jessica stood in place, watching her. "No Wanted poster or timetable for a robbery lying on the ground?"

"Give me a minute." Sophie pictured him running. Snapping her fingers, she said, "When he slipped, I saw something fall. He pushed and pulled at what must be that pile of wood." She pointed to the side of the alley. "They're remodeling inside the jewelry store, so I guess this is the wood and other building supplies that are left over."

They ran over to a stack of scrap plywood and two-by-fours, the same things her parents had used when they did some work on the garage.

Jessica crouched beside the pile. "Hey Sophie, there're some torn-edged papers sticking out from under this board. But it's probably just trash."

Sophie crouched. "No. This makes sense. He must have dropped papers as he tripped. Then they got wedged between pieces of wood when he landed against the pile. He was pushing hard on the stack of wood, but he couldn't seem to shift it. Then it tore." Sophie put her hands on the pile. "Here, help me push against it with all our might."

Jessica crossed her arms and stared at her. "Why would you think a man who must be bigger than us couldn't move it, but we can?"

"He didn't have time to do much." Sophie put her hands on the side of the stack. "Push."

Jessica touched the stack and grimaced. "Yuck. If there's only trash under this sawdust-covered, splinter-filled pile, you owe me a chocolate milkshake."

"Deal. Ready?"

Jessica put her hands against the pile. "Okay."

"Push."

Groaning, they pushed as hard as they could. Nothing happened. "Again." Sophie stood ready. Jessica stepped into position and they pushed. This time, the top of the stack rolled backward, freeing the papers.

Sophie reached down and slid them out from under a board. "Yes! Yes! Yes! Here's the clue we've been waiting for." She waved a stack of papers in the air.

"What's the clue?"

Sophie thumbed through them. "We have a corner of most pages, almost a half page of a couple. They're typed, official-looking papers and newspaper articles." She studied the woodpile, then sighed. "I guess we'd better stack this up like we found it."

A short time later, Sophie stood back and surveyed the stacked pile of scrap lumber. "I think it's neater than when we got here."

Jessica brushed off the front of her shorts. "But we definitely are not."

Walking back to the sheriff's office, Sophie flipped through the papers. "There are ten pieces of paper."

"Can I see?" Jessica leaned over. "Did you actually find a big clue for a real mystery?" When Sophie handed them to her, she stopped to study them. "The typed pages look like official documents. There are words like *wherefore* and *whereas*."

"I know I've heard those words on TV shows and movies with lawyers."

"I don't know if you noticed, but some are from the bottom of a page and some are from the top. And a couple are just small corners." She flipped through them. "You know, Sophie, these might have been stuck between those boards for a week or two."

"Nope." Sophie smiled confidently. "Remember getting soaked yesterday?"

Jessica rocked back on her heels. "Oh yeah. This paper has never been wet." She flipped through them again. "There's only a paragraph or so of each of the two newspaper articles. If we had the whole articles, we might know a great deal about this mystery."

"So you finally admit we've found a mystery."

Jessica pursed her lips. "I don't think I have a choice. If that man was innocent, I don't think he would have run away from a twelve-year-old girl *and* abandoned these papers."

Sophie fingered the pages. This definitely wasn't another feather. "I wonder if there's more than one mystery. Let's see what's going on with the accident in front of the sheriff's office."

A man in a brown suit came around the corner of the next block, walking toward them. Jessica said, "Hey, look at him."

"Who?"

"That man. It's kind of crazy, but I'm getting suspicious of all men in brown suits."

As soon as Sophie focused on him, he did a one-eighty and went back around the corner.

"He's carrying a briefcase like the one we found."

Hurrying after him, they watched him slowly amble past the sheriff's office. Then he abruptly tucked the briefcase under his arm.

"After him!" Sophie called over her shoulder as she raced down the sidewalk with Jessica on her heels. The man darted around the next corner with both girls close behind. Rounding the corner onto Dogwood Street, they came to a stop and found an empty street. "There isn't anyone in sight."

"If we were in the city, there'd be plenty of people to question. We should solve a mystery there."

Sophie could tell that Jessica was starting to enjoy crime solving. "Maybe we'll go to the city for our *next* mystery."

Jessica groaned. "Oh no. What have I said?"

Sophie smiled. "Admit it. You're hooked on mysteries."

Jessica pressed her lips together.

"Not talking, huh?"

Jessica shook her head.

8

Missing Evidence

The cars from the accident were driving away when Jessica and Sophie walked into the sheriff's office. Jessica had already been in this office more times than she'd expected to be in any law enforcement office in her whole life.

Sheriff Valeska entered right after them, took off her hat, threw it onto her desk, and sat down. Leaning back in her chair, she rubbed her eyes, "That was an odd accident."

Sophie sat forward. "Why?"

"The drivers said they saw something go across the street. They swerved to avoid it and hit each other." She pulled a small toy car out of her coat pocket. "When we searched, we found this wind-up car on the sidewalk."

"Diversion," Sophie said with certainty.

Sheriff Valeska laughed. "It's more likely that a child was playing with this toy, and when it went the wrong way and caused an accident, he or she ran away."

Sophie crossed her arms. "We got here just after the accident. I saw a suspicious man go out the back door and down the alley."

"You followed a man?"

Jessica added, "And just now we saw a man in a brown suit carrying a briefcase that looked like the one we found. We followed him too, but he vanished on Dogwood Street."

Sheriff Valeska stood. "I'll see if anything is out of order."

After checking around the office, she said, "Everything seems fine here." Then she went into the room where she'd taken the briefcase the other day. "It's gone!"

"See? I told you, Jessica." Sophie sat proudly, with a smug expression on her face.

"What's gone?" Jessica asked.

"The briefcase." Sophie smiled in a superior manner. "Right, Sheriff?"

The sheriff dropped onto her chair and faced her computer. "It's hard to believe, but our usually overly dramatic Sophie was right." She clicked the mouse a couple of times, then said, "Sophie, tell me every detail you can remember about both incidents. And carefully describe the suspects."

Sophie bounced all over her seat. "I'm part of a crime scene. Let me think. The suspect who went out the back door was wearing a cream-colored dress shirt and . . ." She stopped for a minute. Then her face grew red and she buried her face in her hands. Jessica could barely hear her muffled voice. "I've seen this happen in movies and read about it in books. I thought I'd have a fabulous description, but all I remember is he had on a light-colored dress shirt."

The sheriff encouraged her. "That is a clue. You're sure it was a man?"

"Absolutely." She tapped her foot, then jumped up. "I couldn't see more than his back or side because he held a brown jacket up near his face. I'll bet he did that so I couldn't see him." Placing her hands on the sheriff's desk, she leaned forward. "I do know he had short hair, dark brown or black. What do you think, Jessica?"

The sheriff turned toward Jessica. "You saw him too?"

"Only from a distance when I ran after Sophie. She was chasing him, so she got much closer."

"Sophie chased him?"

Jessica smiled. "A possible villain on the run? What do you think?"

Sophie said, "Yes, I'm sure now. He did have short, dark hair. And then we found the bits of paper that were wedged in the lumber behind Kendall's Jewelers."

"Bits of paper? Did he drop them?"

"I think so."

"Let me see them."

Sophie pulled them out of her pocket and handed them to Sheriff Valeska.

She flipped through the pages. "This looks like trash."

Jessica said, "That's what I thought at first."

The sheriff handed them back to Sophie. "You can keep these."

This surprised Jessica, because even she knew they were important. But Sophie had seen them fall, not the sheriff, and it must be difficult for a sheriff to build a crime around what a kid says. Sophie quickly stuffed them back in her pocket.

Jessica added, "We only caught a glimpse of the man with the briefcase a few minutes ago and could really only see that he was wearing a brown suit."

The sheriff kept working. "We'd dusted the briefcase for fingerprints, then put the feathers back inside. I was going to take it to the crime lab tomorrow when I went to the county seat for a meeting so they could go over it with a fine-tooth comb." She leaned to the right and pulled a file folder out of her drawer, checked something, then continued working at the computer. "On Monday morning I'll need you to bring in the feather you took. It's the only one we have now." She clicked the mouse before adding, "You girls should probably go now."

Sophie patted the pocket with the pieces of paper. "Sure. We'll let you know if we find any other clues."

"Oh, and girls, please don't chase any other strangers."

Sophie stood. "We'll be careful."

When they were walking out the door, Jessica asked Sophie, "Did you call her and tell her about the man at the resort?"

Sophie glared at her.

Uh-oh. I guess not.

The sheriff stopped working and focused on the girls. "What man?"

"The one who asked us about the feathers and chased us through the resort," Jessica answered.

The sheriff pointed at the chairs in front of her desk. "Sit, ladies. Tell me what happened."

Jessica went step-by-step through the incident. "Then we hid in the tunnel behind the waterfall."

"You girls be careful. I don't know what's going on yet, but this feather mystery is one of the strangest things I've ever heard of."

Jessica said, "Don't worry. We will, Sheriff."

As they left, Sophie muttered, "Feather Mystery. So it has a name now." She turned left, so Jessica figured she was headed toward her bench. "Let's solve this mystery."

Jessica laughed. "We haven't even figured out what kind of bird the feather is from. And we don't know if both the feathers and the papers are connected. Sheriff Valeska didn't think so."

Sophie didn't seem to be paying any attention. "I know!" She pointed a finger in the air. "Our mystery is like the last book I read. No, the book before that."

"Hurry up and tell me."

"Something happened, and it seemed like it didn't have anything to do with the mystery, but it turned out to be very important. I really think we need to consider what's going on at Simpson's Shoes. That's the only other mysterious happening in Pine Hill."

"No way. Your mystery thinking is off this time. Like I said before, unlocked doors in a shoe store and a briefcase full of feathers don't have anything in common. We have three things that might not go together at all—feathers, papers, and unlocked doors."

"You'll see." Sophie glanced over at her bench but kept walking. "It's probably time to go home."

When they were at the edge of town, Jessica swatted at a fly buzzing around her head and caught a glimpse of a man behind them. "Ooh, Sophie. A little while ago I looked back and saw a man behind us. He's still there and looks like a suspicious type. Do you think he's following us?"

Sophie started to turn around, but Jessica put out her arm to stop her. "Hey, you're the one who said you have to be casual."

"I'll tie my shoe." She bent over, retied her old sneakers, and glanced behind them.

"What's he wearing?"

"Green shirt. Blue jeans."

"He's the minister from our church. You'll see him again at church tomorrow morning." Sophie grinned and stood. "I think he's okay."

"Whew. I'm glad we're going to be out in the open today. We find a briefcase in the woods and all of a sudden, I'm seeing a bad guy when there's a good guy. This could be a long, long summer."

"You'll love solving mysteries soon."

Jessica didn't say anything to Sophie, but her stay in Pine Hill *had* been exciting.

9

What's Up with Down?

Jessica opened her eyes and blinked a few times. Her cousin's pale pink walls with a painted border of little purple flowers came into focus. She knew Sophie well enough now to be certain she hadn't chosen the pink or the flowers. But the forest green fleece blankets that covered the beds were pure Sophie.

When she rolled over, she found her cousin's bed empty. Jessica walked to the bathroom door and heard the shower running, so she lay back down and picked up her book. The girl in it always got straight A's. What would it be like if people knew she was brainy too? That she easily got straight A's?

Sophie came out of the bathroom wearing a robe, and a towel wrapped around her head.

Jessica said, "Morning, Cousin."

Sophie stared silently at her.

Jessica flipped back her covers. "I think I've been awake long enough that I'm in a good mood, but I'll take a shower before you say anything to me."

Sophie nodded.

As hot water sprayed down on her, Jessica felt more and more awake. By the time she walked back into Sophie's room, she was humming her favorite song. Sophie sat on the end of her bed, already dressed, this time in a less faded pair of jeans and a green T-shirt instead of the usual white. Jessica flipped through her clothes hanging in the closet. Would people at Sophie's church dress the same as they did at hers? She started to ask, then immediately realized that wouldn't work. Sophie wouldn't notice clothes. Jessica settled on a white skirt and a pale pink top.

Jessica stepped over to her beauty station, carefully did her eye makeup, then added blush.

"Do you miss your parents?" Sophie asked.

"Yeah." She chose a soft pink lip gloss.

"I see my dad every day. It must be strange to have your dad gone for months at a time because he's working in a country that's far away."

Jessica pictured running to her dad in the airport the last time he'd come home. "It is. And now Mom's visiting him, so they're both gone." As tears filled her eyes, she sat on her bed with her back to Sophie.

"I have to admit, I didn't want you here and I didn't like you much at first, but you're growing on me."

"Thanks. I think." Jessica smiled at Sophie's awkward way of saying she was starting to like her. She blinked the tears away and sniffed. "I even miss my little brother."

"Do you like him? I've always wanted a brother."

"He's constantly in the way, but I guess I'm used to having Frog Boy around."

"Frog Boy?"

"Yeah, when he was a baby, Dad called him 'our tadpole.' I knew a tadpole was a frog, so I called him Frog." Feeling a little less sad, Jessica turned to Sophie and smiled. "I'm the only one who's allowed to call him that."

Sophie grinned. "Even you might not get away with it when he's our age."

Jessica went over to the closet, chose a pair of white sandals from her shoes on the floor, and slipped them on. "I'm ready for church. Do you have any ideas for afterward?"

"I'd love to get out in the woods again. How about another hike on Cutoff Trail?" Sophie practically bounced, she was so excited.

Jessica cringed. She still had an image in her mind of owls and bats hovering overhead, ready to swoop down. "Can we go somewhere that's not so filled with nature?"

"Well, getting in the middle of nature is usually my first choice, but . . . deal." Sophie sat silently. "It's so sunny and beautiful today that we should go somewhere outside. I know. I could give you a tour of Pine Hill. We might see a person or place that helps us solve The Feather Mystery." Sophie's eyes lit up whenever she talked about the mystery. She made it difficult to *not* be excited about it. "Maybe later we could study the papers for clues."

"Since I didn't want to study them last night, today works." Jessica flopped back on her bed. "We're going to end up using all of our summer vacation to solve this."

Sophie laughed. "Sounds like fun to me." She put her feet into her usual sneakers. "We'd better grab some breakfast so we'll be ready to go."

Sophie's dad stepped into the kitchen a little later. "Ready, girls?"

"Ready," Sophie answered.

A short drive took them to a brick church—what else?—on the other side of town that, other than the bricks, reminded Jessica of her own church. It was hard not to miss her family on Sunday morning. They would go to church together every week, her dad joining them when he was in town. Not a single part of her normal life existed here. Jessica bit her cheek so she wouldn't cry.

As the minister stepped up to the pulpit, she scooted closer to Sophie and whispered, "Please *do not* tell him I thought he looked like a criminal." That humiliation would be too much to take today.

Sophie hesitated, then nodded.

Halfway through the service, a boy a few rows up turned his head to the side, and Jessica's heart caught in her throat. *Tony comes here!* She liked knowing he believed the same things she did.

After church, Aunt April and Uncle Lucas dropped the girls off in front of Great Finds, her aunt's antique shop, because it was, her aunt said, "centrally located." The shop was closed for the day, but Jessica looked in the window and saw a room filled with furniture and small things—she guessed all old things, like those in Sophie's house.

"Okay. Tour time," Sophie said.

They went over to Sophie's school, a building less than half the size of her own, and they peered into the windows of Sophie's science classroom (she'd had a fun teacher last year), the cafeteria, and the library. Walking through town after that, Sophie turned a corner, onto a street Jessica hadn't seen before.

Jessica glanced into the shop windows as they walked by, stopping in front of a flower shop called Buds & Blooms. She peered into the window. "Mom loves flowers."

Sophie said, "Mine too. I haven't been around here in a while." She turned in a circle, scanning the stores. "Hey, that's Mrs. Bowman from Bananas." She pointed to a woman standing by the front door of a shop across the street. "It's funny that she's here, because she's blocks from her business and even farther from her house. I guess she went shopping in that store."

"She isn't carrying anything."

"True. And she seems to be in a hurry."

The older woman crossed the street and quickly moved out of sight.

"I don't remember what used to be in that store, but I know it's different now. The sign above the door says, 'The Down Shoppe.' Down what?"

Jessica shrugged. "Probably like a fluffy down comforter or down coat that keeps you warm in the winter."

"Fluffy?"

"You know. They're filled with feathers."

"Feathers!" both girls shouted.

They hurried across the street, and Sophie and Jessica stared into the store window.

"'The Down Shoppe' is such a perfect clue." Sophie craned her neck, trying to see inside. They may have made the breakthrough in the mystery that she needed.

"The window display is empty. And more than a little dusty. I wouldn't shop here unless they cleaned the place up."

Sophie cupped her hands and held them against the glass. "I can see farther into the store now."

Jessica copied her. "There isn't anything in there. You know, Sophie, the Down Shoppe might only have feathers *in* things. Not loose feathers, like in the briefcase."

"Maybe." Sophie walked over to the glass front door, then muttered, "Still nothing. And a sign says they don't open for another three weeks." She banged on the door.

Jessica jumped. "Hey!"

"I see a woman in there."

A woman with long brown hair crept slowly toward the door. Dressed in worn overalls and a yellow T-shirt with a huge flower pin on the shoulder strap, she would be hard to miss in a crowd. Keeping her head down, the woman pointed at the sign on the door and stopped when she was about five feet away.

"We need to talk to you," Sophie called out.

"We?" the woman said loudly from behind the closed door.

She wasn't making sense.

Then Jessica said, "*Parlez-vous anglais?*"

The woman shook her head from side to side.

"Thank you. *Merci.*"

She raced to the back of the room and out of sight.

As Sophie started to speak, Jessica said, "'We' is actually *o-u-i* and means 'yes' in French. I asked her if she spoke English."

Sophie's brow wrinkled. "I guess that means you speak French?"

"We lived in the south of France during some of those years you and I didn't see each other."

Sophie hit her forehead with the palm of her hand. "Yeah, now I remember Christmas cards coming from a cousin I didn't know who lived far away."

"Yep. That was me." She cocked her head to the side and tapped her foot on the ground. "There was something odd about that woman . . . I just can't figure out what."

"I know I couldn't identify her later. Her hair almost covered her face."

"True," Jessica muttered.

Sophie pushed on Jessica's arm. "What do you want to do now?"

Jessica shrugged. "Now I would like to do something that is absolutely not related to this mystery. You're from here, Miss Pine Hill. What would be fun?"

Fun would be camping, or a hike in the woods, but Sophie knew Jessica would not like those ideas. What would be outside that Jessica wouldn't mind? "Let's walk down to the lake."

They went down a slight hill on a paved path that wove through pine trees. Then they stepped out of the trees, and the lake sat in front of them. Sophie never got tired of seeing it. A bright, sunny Sunday had brought out boats of all sizes.

"Wow! This lake is beautiful. And enormous. With an awesome sandy beach." Jessica turned first to the right, then to the left. "Hey, Cousin, why haven't you taken me to this un-woodsy place before?"

"I showed you Pine Lake your first day here. Remember? From Cutoff Trail?"

Jessica winced. "Guess I didn't pay attention to the lake."

A boat roared by, pulling someone on water skis.

Turning to Sophie, Jessica said, "We have to come back to this beach when we're wearing bathing suits."

"Sounds good. Um, you know, Jessica, I've been thinking. We have to investigate the Down Shoppe."

"Not the mystery again. You won't relax until we solve this." Jessica took a few steps toward the water, then turned to Sophie. "Okay, I'll be the voice of reason again. You're pulling in unrelated things and calling them clues. The Down Shoppe might have nothing to do with the briefcase."

"But they have feathers in there."

Jessica raised one eyebrow. "Would a jewelry store automatically be part of a crime if someone had found a briefcase full of gold?"

"Maybe." Sophie grinned.

Jessica grinned back. "We'll see. What was it about that woman?" She stared out at the lake. "Where to now, Cousin?"

"I'm hungry. Let's go home and help Mom make dinner." Sophie took a couple of steps, then let out a little whoop. "I just remembered that I recorded an old detective movie the other day. It might give us some mystery-solving ideas."

10

Ouch!

After they'd done some chores the next morning, including vacuuming and dusting—the dusting an extra Sophie said she hoped would earn points with her mom—Jessica sat down on the couch in the living room. She hoped, but it was probably too much to ask, that they wouldn't do something mystery-related today.

Sophie plopped onto the couch. "What would a world-famous detective do right now?"

Yes, it was too much to ask.

Sophie sprang to her feet. "Read through the papers. There *must* be clues hiding in them."

Sophie hurried into her bedroom, Jessica following, since she knew Sophie wouldn't let it go. When she'd removed the metal box from its hiding place, she took the papers out and placed them on her bed in a single layer.

They both sat on the edge of the bed and went through them one by one.

Jessica didn't find the few sentences from the newspaper articles very useful. "One talks about coats and sleeping bags and another about tourism. And we only have a little more of the official-looking papers, which, like you said earlier, use words lawyers use, like *whereas*. We can't even tell if any of these have something to do with Pine Hill. Maybe they are just trash." She flopped back on the bed. "We don't know a whole lot more than we did a half hour ago. This is just like the feathers."

Sophie picked up the ten pieces of paper and slowly went through them. "Since we're losing the feather, maybe there's a way to learn more about the papers. I understand the words in the newspaper articles, but the typed, official-looking pages are different. Not only are there words I don't know, there are long strings of numbers and letters too. Trying to read these is worse than reading something for language arts class. In fact, it's even worse than social studies." She threw the papers down on the bed.

Jessica picked them up. She might not be able to figure out what each page was about, and she sure didn't understand the letters and numbers together, but she did know almost all of the words. They didn't come together to mean anything though.

"You seem to understand what you're reading," Sophie exclaimed.

"What?" Jessica looked up from the last page, blinked, and paused. Had she given herself away? "Um, you can read all the words. It's a matter of understanding them."

"You're right. There for a minute, I thought you really understood what you were reading." Sophie took the papers out of Jessica's hand. "I wanted to solve this myself, but my dad usually has good ideas about these things. Let's take the official-looking pages to him." She headed down the hall to his office, then paused. "The door's closed." She shifted from foot to foot.

"Are you allowed to knock?"

After a few seconds, Sophie reached up and gently tapped on the door. Jessica hoped she wouldn't get in trouble.

"Yes?" Uncle Lucas called.

"We have a question for you."

"Come on in."

"Whew." Sophie said as she reached for the doorknob. "Does he usually get mad if you knock?"

"I *usually* leave him alone to work. He's an accountant, so he has to keep track of a lot of numbers." Sophie started to push the door open. "He says the only way to focus on his work in the summer with a chatterbox like me around is to close the door."

Jessica grinned as they walked inside. Sophie handed the papers to her dad and told him how they'd found them—minus the part about chasing the guy.

"They're pages from a legal document," Uncle Lucas said as soon as he'd paged through them.

Sophie wrinkled her forehead. "We noticed the words lawyers use."

"Don't ask me any more than that. You need to talk to a lawyer." He reached for the phone and dialed, then said, "Sara Samuels, please."

Jessica tapped her foot and checked out her uncle's office. He had a nice computer. Too bad Sophie couldn't use it.

"Sara? Lucas Sandoval here. My daughter and niece found some pages from a legal document and want to know more about them. Could they bring them in for a quick legal review? I'm sure two o'clock will be fine. Thanks."

Sophie kissed her father on the cheek as he was hanging up the phone. "Thanks, Dad."

"The office is at Oak Street and Acadia Avenue, on the other side of town." He got one of those stern parent looks. "The two of you need to be on time."

"We will, Uncle Lucas. Um, I know Sophie doesn't use your computer, but could I use it morning or night to send a message to Mom and Dad? We were going to text, but you can't do that here. Then they said they'd call every few days instead, but—"

"Of course. Come in tonight and write to them."

"Thank you." Jessica closed the door and sighed. Being able to communicate with her mom every day would make a summer in Pine Hill *much* easier to survive.

After a quick sandwich, the girls headed to Sophie's room. Jessica studied her clothes in the closet, pulling out a couple of outfits and laying them on the bed. "You know, Sophie, I think you're supposed to dress nicely when you go to see a lawyer."

"Hmm. Like a fancy restaurant?"

"Something like that."

"I've only been to a couple fancy restaurants. Mostly the resort." Sophie flipped through her smaller amount of clothes on hangers—most of her clothes were T-shirts and jeans lying in drawers—then eyed the shoes Jessica had neatly placed on the closet floor. "Women wear high heels when they dress up."

"They often do," Jessica said. Should she go with the pants or the skirt? Pants.

"Can I wear a pair of your high heels?"

Jessica whipped around. "What? It must be a long walk to the other side of town. Have you ever worn high heels?"

"No, but I want to give it a try," Sophie pleaded. "I can picture myself stepping into a lawyer's office wearing a beautiful dress and high heels. I know that's how the lawyer will be dressed."

From wearing sneakers, even to church, to high heels? And walking a long distance? This had 'bad idea' written all over it. Jessica tried to throw her off. "Sophie, I don't know if we wear the same size shoe."

Sophie glanced from her feet to Jessica's. "I think we're pretty much the same size. How about if I take my normal shoes in a tote bag?"

"Well . . ." Jessica paused. "That seems to make sense. Then you can change if you need to." Jessica pulled a pair of black high heels out of the closet and set them on the floor by Sophie's bed. "Even if these do fit, I think you're going to regret this. But they'll go with almost anything, and the heel is low enough that these are probably the easiest I have for you to walk in."

Sophie startled her by taking a beautiful teal dress out of the closet and slipping it on. "This is my best dress. My mother said I would need it someday." She shrugged. "Might as well wear it now."

When she reached for the shoes, Jessica stepped between her and them. "You know, it took me a while to learn how to walk in high heels. And I was on flat ground in the city."

Sophie grinned and reached around her for the shoes. Trying them on, she exclaimed, "They fit. We wear the same shoe size."

Jessica didn't think Sophie would be as happy about that later. Turning, she checked out her own appearance in the mirror. The black pants and white blouse came off as professional but not over-the-top. Then she thought about her choice of shoes. Sneakers would work for the walk. She'd put heels on when she got to the lawyer's office.

She picked up her purse, slipped her cell phone out of its pocket, and set it on the dresser. Good reception seemed to be limited to times when she really didn't need a phone. Then she picked the phone back up. With everything that was going on, it might come in handy.

Sophie put the papers into a surprisingly cute denim tote bag. When they got to the door, she turned back, tottering a little on the heels.

Jessica hoped she'd come back wearing sneakers, but she just returned holding up their feather.

"We'd better drop this off on the way," Sophie said. She tucked the feather into the bag and they started off, Sophie walking slowly but steadily.

Jessica kept an eye on her, keeping to the edge of the paved road for the smoothest path to town. By the outskirts of Pine Hill, Sophie was walking tenderly, putting more pressure on her left foot. A block from the sheriff's office, she began wincing when she put down her right foot.

Jessica gently pushed Sophie in the direction of her favorite bench. "Sit here and I'll run the feather in to the sheriff."

When Sophie quietly sat as she'd asked, Jessica knew she wasn't herself.

Jessica took the feather out of Sophie's bag, then into the sheriff's office. She found the sheriff seated at her desk and held out the feather to her.

Tucking it into an envelope, Sheriff Valeska asked, "Where's Sophie?"

"She's learning to walk in high heels, so she's resting on a bench outside."

The sheriff's eyebrows shot upward. "Sophie? Is she okay?"

"I hope so," Jessica answered, turning to leave. Almost out the door, she turned back. "I know she'll ask later if we can see the feather if we want to."

The sheriff wrote something on the envelope before she answered. "I agree that she will ask. Tell her I'll consider it and that I'm starting to realize there's more to this mystery than I'd thought."

Jessica walked back to Sophie. She knew her cousin would love hearing that. But right now she didn't think it would register with the brain of the girl on the bench, staring blankly straight ahead.

11

Legal Matters

Jessica and Sophie continued on, Sophie now giving a little hop each time she took a step. By the time they arrived at the two-story building the lawyer's office was in—thankfully, on time—Sophie was almost dragging one foot and then the other. But she hadn't complained. Actually, she hadn't said a word in about twenty minutes. She just had a stupid grin on her face.

Jessica sat down in the lobby and slipped off her sneakers, trading them for high-heeled, tan strappy sandals she'd brought in a pink tote bag. Then she got up and they followed the sign with an arrow that led them down the hall to the lawyer's office, and Jessica told the secretary why they were there. Sophie kept that stupid grin the whole time.

While they sat on a sofa and waited for the lawyer to finish with her previous appointment, Jessica studied Sophie, who was definitely breathing but not moving otherwise. Could painful feet hurt you in other ways? "Sophie?"

Sophie turned toward her.

"You okay?"

"I think so," she said softly.

The phone on the secretary's desk rang. After speaking on it, she quickly ushered the girls through a door to her right and into an office.

A woman wearing an elegant red business suit with black high heels stood beside a desk. Sophie nudged Jessica with her elbow. Her expression said, *I was right. Lawyers dress in beautiful clothes.*

Sophie dug the papers out of her tote bag and handed them to the lawyer. "Do you have any idea what these mean?"

"Please sit down, ladies."

As the girls sat in the padded leather chairs in front of the desk, Mrs. Samuels walked around the desk and sat down. Reading the papers one by one, she nodded her head. At one point her brow wrinkled. She entered something into her computer, then went back and forth repeatedly, comparing that to one of the pieces of paper. When she'd read through all of them, she said, "There's only enough here to know that this is a real estate contract."

"A what?" Jessica asked.

"Someone wants to buy property. What I have here appears to be a standard agreement to do that."

Jessica saw Sophie's face fall.

"There's nothing strange here?" Sophie asked.

Mrs. Samuels flipped back to one of the pages. "There is one 'strange' thing, as you put it. There is what's called a legal address on one piece of paper. That's the series of numbers and letters. Every house, business, or vacant piece of land has a different one. I've been your parents' lawyer, Sophie, for so many years that it seemed familiar, so I checked and it's for the building Great Finds is in, your mother's shop."

Sophie wrinkled her brow. "Do you mean someone wants to buy Mom's shop?"

Mrs. Samuels said, "It would seem so. Has she mentioned anything about this?"

"No. Not a word."

Mrs. Samuels stood and handed the papers back to Sophie. "That's about it, ladies. I hope I've helped."

"Thank you very much for speaking with us." Sophie stood, wincing as she put weight on her feet and immediately grabbed hold of the desk.

The lawyer rushed around it and steadied Sophie before Jessica even had a chance to stand. "Are you all right?"

Sophie, her face bright red, said, "New shoes."

"Ah." Mrs. Samuels nodded and looked down. "Very pretty."

Sophie turned and walked very carefully through the doorway as the lawyer and Jessica watched. She vanished out of sight, but Jessica knew it would take her a long time to reach the chairs in the lobby.

Mrs. Samuels said, "You should get her to take those shoes off and put her feet up."

Jessica liked the woman. "I know. She wouldn't listen before." Jessica leaned to the right and could see that the secretary had stepped away from her desk, so maybe Mrs.

Samuels had a few minutes. "Can I ask you what some of these words mean?"

The lawyer seemed surprised. "Sure."

Jessica asked about a few of them and listened carefully as Mrs. Samuels explained the meanings.

"You have an amazing command of language for someone so young. Have you thought about being a lawyer?"

"Sometimes. I'm not sure what I want to be." Jessica heard the door to the office open and close. "Thank you."

She passed the secretary as she left and found Sophie sitting in a chair in the lobby, with her sneakers on her feet and the high heels on the floor. She stood when Jessica neared.

"Oh boy, when you are right, Cousin, you are right." Sophie grabbed the high heels and stuffed them in her bag. "Whew, my feet still hurt. But not like with those instruments of torture. How can you wear them?"

Jessica laughed. "First, I'm used to them. Second, as I mentioned when you weren't paying attention, this is a long walk in heels. I wore sneakers."

"I heard you. But I figured *I* could do it. I thought that if I could run up Cutoff Trail, I could walk across town in high heels."

"It isn't the same."

"Tell me about it."

"Let's go home. I'm curious what your mom will say tonight about the real estate deal."

Sophie walked slowly out the door, limping each time her right foot touched the ground, and saying, "Ouch" each time her left one did.

"I think it's going to take a while to get home," Jessica muttered to herself as she followed Sophie out the door.

When they got to the corner of the block, Jessica checked her watch. Ten minutes just to get there.

A car pulled around the corner and the driver, who turned out to be Mrs. Samuels, rolled down the window. "Can I give you ladies a ride?"

Jessica pulled out her phone. "Three bars." She gave a thumbs-up and handed it to Sophie. "Call your parents first."

Dialing, Sophie said quietly, "They'll be fine with it." A minute later she hung up. "Let's go."

As Sophie slid into the backseat, Jessica gratefully opened the car door and climbed into the front seat. If they'd had to walk home, tonight's dinner would have been about ten o'clock—tomorrow morning.

Aunt April served burgers and fries. When her aunt went into the kitchen to get dessert, Jessica waited for something exciting, like strawberry shortcake, but she returned with the not-so-exciting bowl of fruit.

Sophie nudged her and whispered, "Go get the papers." Jessica was about to ask why she couldn't do it herself when Sophie raised her feet and wiggled them.

After running to get the papers, Jessica handed them to Sophie, then grabbed the peach she'd had her eyes on.

"Mom, are you selling your shop?" Sophie asked.

Mrs. Sandoval paused, with her apple half-peeled. "A man offered to buy my building and my inventory today. Where did *you* get the idea?"

"Remember the papers the thief dropped in the alley?"

"I know your overactive imagination believes there's a thief." Mrs. Sandoval smiled at the girls, then continued peeling.

"You'll believe in the mystery when you read this." Sophie handed her mom the pieces of paper.

Jessica added, "Mrs. Samuels says these papers, or at least some of them, are part of a contract to buy the Great Finds building."

Mrs. Sandoval flipped through them. "It's hard to tell that from what's written here. I'll take Sara Samuels' word for it, though. To answer your question, I have no plans to sell Great Finds." As she set the papers down, she said, "I have a question for you. Did you give away the whipped cream?"

"Huh?" Sophie stared at her mother.

"I noticed the other day that all of the whipped cream was gone, so I wondered if you'd given it to the neighbors. Jessica said we had enough for us *and* them."

"Uh, no." Sophie looked over at Jessica with a giveaway, panicked expression.

They'd forgotten to buy whipped cream to replace what they'd used. Uncle Lucas had warned them.

"We did use quite a bit that night. Um, did I tell you I wore high heels today?"

Sophie'd handled that diversion well. Thinking about her in high heels would be enough to throw anyone off, and it did.

Mrs. Sandoval dropped a slice of apple, then sat with her mouth open for a minute. She said, "I guess you tried on a pair of Jessica's to see what they were like."

"Sophie walked to the lawyer's office in them." Jessica giggled. "'Walked' might be exaggerating. She hopped and dragged herself to the lawyer's office."

Sophie glared at her.

Mrs. Sandoval exclaimed, "Oh, Sophie, your feet must be hurting."

Sophie moved a foot and winced. "Let's just say that it will be a while before I try high heels again. Maybe you can check out my feet after dinner?"

"Of course." Mrs. Sandoval put her hand on Sophie's shoulder. "There does seem to be something mysterious going on in Pine Hill. Be careful. Don't take any chances. Both of you."

"We won't, Aunt April." Jessica thought about the feather they'd given to the sheriff, and the papers. No matter how hard it was to believe, they'd landed right in the middle of a real mystery.

12

A Mysterious Woman

Ring.

Sophie blinked awake, then started to roll over.

Ring.

"It's the phone," Jessica said into her pillow.

"Dad'll get it." Sophie stretched and yawned.

On the fourth ring Sophie leaped to her feet and ran for the phone in the living room. "Dad must not be in his office," she called behind her.

"Okay, Mom," Sophie said into the phone, moments later. Then after a pause, "Yes, we'll be there soon."

She hung up and came back to the bedroom. "When the phone rang, I hoped it was someone with a clue." She laughed. "Of course, who would call with a clue? Anyway, Mom wants us to come to her shop and deliver something."

"In case you forgot to be afraid of me in the morning, I think I'm waking up nicer. Maybe it's all the exercise."

Sophie raised an eyebrow. "I *had* forgotten that I shouldn't talk to you."

Jessica sat up. "I *am* better."

Laughing, Sophie said, "I'm still afraid to talk to you, in case grumpy Jessica returns."

"I think I'll have a good morning. Beach later?"

"Absolutely."

They showered and ate, then dressed with bathing suits under their clothes. Sophie put her shoes on when they were ready to leave, and winced. "Ouch." She went to the medicine cabinet, got two bandages, and covered her two blisters, one on each foot. Then she put her shoes on again. Letting out a big sigh, she said, "So much better."

Leaving, Sophie went in the direction of the shortcut through the woods.

Jessica stopped. "With the guy in the brown suit *and* the guy asking about feathers out there, I'd like to stay by the road."

Sophie didn't want to say so, but Jessica was right. She turned back toward the road. "It'll take longer. There's a gravel path beside it so we don't have to walk where the cars go."

They walked side by side for a while. Then Sophie thought she heard something behind them, so stopped.

Jessica, now a few feet ahead of her, looked back. "Hey. What's the idea?"

"Shh." Sophie held her finger to her lips.

A crunching sound came from somewhere behind them. After a few seconds, it stopped. Jessica walked back to her.

"I think someone's following us," Sophie whispered.

Jessica rolled her eyes, then in a normal voice said, "A criminal followed the detective in that old movie we watched."

Sophie glared at her, then whispered, "I can prove this. Walk."

When they'd taken four steps, the crunching started again. They stopped and it stopped a few seconds later. Sophie and Jessica looked at each other.

Sophie whispered. "You know, this road has so many curves in it that we wouldn't see someone who's close to us."

"Let's do it again."

Sophie hoped she would *only* hear birds singing. They were too far from her house to cut through the woods and run back.

As soon as they started walking, the crunching began. When they stopped, the crunching stopped. Stuff like this only happened in books and movies.

Jessica whispered, "I'll call the sheriff." She pulled her cell phone out of her purse. "No reception." As she put the phone away, the crunching started again.

"Run!" Sophie yelled.

Racing toward town, Sophie felt her heart pounding. She wouldn't admit it to anyone, but having someone follow them had scared her. Sophie whipped around the corner of the first street in Pine Hill, her cousin right on her tail.

Jessica called out, "Stop. No one's behind us."

Sophie pushed her heels into the sidewalk. Jessica swerved to miss her and stopped.

Panting, they sat on the curb. Sophie looked up to realize she was directly across the street from the Down Shoppe. "Strange that a mysterious pursuer would chase us right back to the Down Shoppe."

Jessica leaped to her feet. "I've got it!"

Sophie jumped. "Ooh, you startled me. What?"

"The French woman, and I use that phrase loosely, shook her head to say no."

"And?"

"The French shrug." Jessica raised her shoulders to demonstrate. "They don't shake their heads to say no, like Americans do. Something's fishy at the feather place."

Sophie grinned. "Good work. Let's take another peek."

This time, when they peered through the windows, there wasn't even a person in the room.

Sophie tilted her head to the side. "I know a little about business because Mom and Dad both own their own businesses and they talk about them. I think people should be working here to turn this into a real store if they want to open in a few weeks."

"That makes sense."

Jessica sat down on the curb again, and Sophie paced back and forth between the corner and the front of the Down Shoppe. She stopped and stared at the building.

"We'd better get to your mom's shop."

"Yeah. The sooner we get there, the sooner we're at the beach."

They walked a couple of blocks to Great Finds. "You haven't seen the inside. Be prepared for a lot of really old stuff."

Her mom was arranging items on a shelf toward the back. Sophie walked her cousin around the shop.

"You're right," Jessica whispered. "I've never seen so many old things in one place. Furniture, plates, vases, even a case with jewelry. Some of it's kind of pretty."

"She does like them."

The bell at the front of the store rang, and Sophie ushered Jessica into the back room. "Mom wants it to be peaceful in the store. Unless I'm in the middle of a project, she likes me to be in the back when customers come in because she says I can be 'a disruptive influence.'"

"You sure have been in my life. I never would have gone hunting for a mystery." Jessica sat on the one stool, so Sophie leaned against the wall.

"You know, I thought my brother was going to have the exciting summer, going out with Uncle Bill on his fishing charter boat."

Sophie heard the door's bell ring again.

"You can come out now, girls."

As soon as they entered the room, her mother said, "Over here, Soph. Arms out."

Mrs. Sandoval set a huge box in her arms. Sophie could barely see around the side of the thing.

"Sorry, Soph. I hadn't realized how big it would seem in your arms."

Sophie pulled away when, out of the corner of her eye, she saw her reach for it. "I can carry it. But, Jessica, you're going to have to help guide me."

Mrs. Sandoval said, "Okay, if you can do it, take it to the high school. The mayor's wife called this morning and asked if I could give something for a charity raffle today."

Sophie said, "Don't people normally ask earlier?"

"Always. She told me that the owners of a fishing supply store had promised her something a while back, I think she said a fishing pole, but they're out of town."

Jessica took hold of Sophie's arm and steered her out the door. With her head to the right side of the box, she had a narrow area of vision.

Outside, a man in a brown suit stopped, staring in Great Finds' direction. Was he the same man they'd seen before? A woman wearing a flowered dress and a hat with matching flowers walked in his direction, then seemed to hesitate when she saw him. Had he just shaken his head at her? The woman speeded up, passed him, turned left at the corner, and disappeared out of sight. Then the man glanced around and went around the same corner.

"Jessica, I just saw the strangest thing. Get me to the school and I'll tell you about it." Sophie gave directions from behind the box, then let her cousin lead her.

Sophie's arms were very tired when Jessica said, "I'm happy to report that we've actually arrived at a high school."

After handing the box to the mayor's wife, Sophie shook out her arms. "Whew. I'm glad I didn't have to carry that any longer." She rubbed her upper arms. "Let me tell you what I saw."

Jessica listened, then asked, "So you think they knew each other?"

"It seemed like they did." Sophie shrugged. "Maybe."

On the way to the beach, they went up the street with the Down Shoppe. Sophie thought about the last time they'd looked inside and wondered if maybe Jessica was right, and there wasn't a connection with their mystery.

"Hey." Jessica pointed to the building. "The Down Shoppe has something in their window."

13

Feather Finders

Sophie and Jessica stood in front of the Down Shoppe and stared at the window.

"Sophie," Jessica squeaked, "there are feathers and fluffy white things in this store window."

"It's like what was in the briefcase."

They looked at each other, then back at their surprising find in the store window.

"Get down." Sophie pushed Jessica's head down, and they crouched under the window. "I thought I saw movement in the back of the shop. This might be important. We'd better tell the sheriff."

"Agreed. Let's get to her as fast as we can."

They squatted and hopped for a few feet until they were away from the window, then stood and took off running.

"Sheriff Valeska," Sophie called out as they burst into the sheriff's office.

A deputy sheriff jumped. "She isn't here, Sophie."

"Where can we find her?" Sophie asked, panting.

"She's working. Can I leave her a message?" He picked a sheet of paper up off his desk and walked over to a file cabinet against the wall.

"Tell her we found the feathers."

The deputy turned toward them. "The feathers from the briefcase? Where?"

Jessica said, "They're in the window display of the new Down Shoppe on Olympic Street."

He chuckled. "They're supposed to have feathers in their window display."

Sophie didn't think he understood at all what this meant. And she didn't particularly like being laughed at. "But they're the same kind."

"I know you want to help. I'll leave her the message." The deputy opened a drawer in the file cabinet and dropped the paper in a folder.

Sophie couldn't think of anything else that would convince him. Trudging over to the door, with a deflated Jessica close behind, she pulled it open and ran headfirst into Sheriff Valeska.

The three of them jumped back, the sheriff's hat flying off her head. As Sheriff Valeska reached for it and pushed it back on, she asked. "Do you need something?"

"We have to show you what we found. Please come." Sophie tugged on her arm.

The sheriff cocked her head to the side, then shrugged and followed along.

"We found an important clue. Just around the corner." As they crossed the street, Sophie asked, "Have you learned more about the toy from the accident?"

"There are an adult's fingerprints on the toy, but we don't have a match for them."

"So you have more clues but no answers," Jessica said. "Will you be able to figure out whose fingerprints they are?"

"We sent both them and those from the briefcase to the FBI and hope to have a match soon. I also want you girls to bring in those papers tomorrow so I can make a copy. I'll keep the originals and have someone go over them for clues, even though I don't think it's going to lead anywhere."

When they stopped in front of the Down Shoppe, Sophie swept her hand toward the window like a game show host. "See what we found?"

The sheriff frowned. "I see an empty window display."

Sophie whirled around to the window. "We saw a pile of feathers mixed with white fluffy things, just like those in the briefcase, right here."

"Are you sure they were the same?"

"Exactly," Jessica said.

All traces of their amazing clue had disappeared, and blue fabric was in its place. Pointing at the shop window, Sophie said, "Get a search warrant. Those feathers are in there."

"Sophie, I can't get a search warrant without evidence of a crime."

Sophie put her hands on her face. "But we saw them. They weren't there this morning. Then they were there a few minutes ago, and now they're gone again."

"I believe you, but as far as I know, you're the only ones who noticed them. The feathers have to be in the window display for me to even have a chance of getting a search warrant."

"They must be criminals." Sophie pressed her face to the window. "How else can you explain the feathers being there, then disappearing?"

"They decided to change the display because every time they opened the door, the air coming inside blew white things around the room," Jessica suggested.

"Hey, I thought you were on my side."

"I am. But it is possible."

"Yeah. But it isn't likely. Sheriff, can we at least knock and ask about the feathers?"

"Yes, we can. But they don't have to answer." Sheriff Valeska knocked on the glass door.

Sophie was sure she saw a shadow move in the back of the shop for just a second, but then nothing stirred.

"I'll have one of my deputies drive by here every once in a while."

"Thanks."

Sophie wasn't happy as she trudged away. Jessica tugged on her arm. "There isn't anything else we can do about this now, right?"

"I don't think so."

"Then we've done enough crime-solving. Ready for sun, sand, and water lapping on the shore?"

Sophie perked up. "The beach!"

Jessica pumped air with her fist.

"This is gorgeous." Jessica stretched out on her beach towel and stared at the sky through her sunglasses. "A soft, sandy beach, blue sky, and water. What more could I ask for?"

Sophie rubbed on sunscreen. "You've been to a beach before."

"Not one I could walk to anytime I wanted for a whole summer. This is great."

"I think I know something that could make it even better for you."

Jessica closed her eyes and sighed. "What?"

"Tony."

"Where?" Jessica shot straight up and looked around.

"Try to be a little more subtle. He's over there." Sophie nodded to her right.

Jessica lowered her sunglasses to see more clearly. "He's cute. But I don't know anything about him. I might not even like him if we talk about more than sandwiches."

Sophie laughed. "He's a nice guy."

Just as Sophie spoke, Tony started walking their way. Jessica ran her fingers through her hair. "How do I look?" she whispered.

"Superb," Sophie whispered back.

"Hi, Soph." Tony nudged Sophie to the side and sat beside her on her towel.

"And you remember my cousin."

"Jessica," he said.

Jessica's heart pounded at the thought that he'd remembered *her* name. "Thank you for remembering."

He gave Sophie a crooked smile. "In a town this small, you know everyone's name."

"Oh." Jessica was disappointed. She'd thought he knew her name because he was interested in her. It was a good thing that she had these sunglasses to hide behind.

"I'd better get back to work." Tony stood and brushed sand off his pants.

"Mom will probably have us in Great Finds soon. We'll come over for lunch then."

"Great." He turned toward Jessica. "Do you like ice cream?"

Jessica nodded.

"I'll give each of you a sundae next time." He walked away but looked back when he was almost to the street. The girls waved at him before he turned toward the deli and disappeared out of sight.

"Wow," Sophie exclaimed.

"Wow what?"

"He asked you if you like ice cream, and then he said he'd give us some."

"So? What's your point, Cousin?"

"He's never given me anything free. And I've known him most of my life."

Jessica grinned. "Do you think Aunt April will ask us to help in her shop soon?"

"Maybe we'll volunteer."

"Excellent! I guess he doesn't mind braces." Jessica lay back on her beach towel. When she thought about Tony and the sundaes, she started grinning. She was still grinning when they packed their towels away and started for home.

After dinner, they sat on the couch, Jessica with the newspaper and Sophie with a magazine. Aunt April and Uncle Lucas had taken cups of coffee out onto the front porch after dinner to enjoy the evening, her uncle said.

Jessica said, "You know, Sophie, we could go to the newspaper office and read whatever they've written about the Down Shoppe. It's a new business, so there must be something."

"Mr. Avinson, the owner of the *Pine Hill Press*, is a nice man, so I'll bet he will find us exactly what we need."

Sophie asked her parents if she could call the newspaper owner to see if he would help them. They agreed, and Sophie quickly had him on the line. A few seconds later, she hung up the phone.

"Are we on for tomorrow?"

"No. He's going to be out of town for a couple of days, so we can't meet him until Friday."

"Too bad." Maybe the mystery would leave them alone until then. A summer filled with mysteries wasn't what Jessica had expected when she came to Pine Hill, but Tony was making things better and better.

The next day, Aunt April quickly agreed to their helping at Great Finds. The upside was that Jessica might get to see Tony. The downside was that "helping" meant dusting. She swept a feather duster over things on low shelves, on high shelves, and around the edges of furniture.

At one point, she and Sophie worked near each other. Jessica brushed the duster over small antiques on a shelf and glanced around. "Sophie, there's a lot of empty space on these shelves. Doesn't your mom want to have more to sell?"

"Summer's always busy so there'll be more and more empty space. Mom takes trips in the winter to buy things for the next summer. This year, she's going to Paris." Sophie sighed deeply. "She went a couple of years ago and met up with your mom there."

"You should try talking her into taking you this time." London was a short trip away from there, so they could have a day or two together in Paris while her aunt shopped.

"Don't think I haven't tried. She said that I need to get better grades in my native language before she'll take me to a country where they speak another language."

Jessica laughed, then paused. Sophie didn't know just how good she was at English or French. Or most other subjects. With them living so far apart, she probably wouldn't want her for a tutor anyway. Her secret could stay safely locked away—and she could stay guilt-free for not offering.

Jessica hoped for a trip to the deli for lunch, but Aunt April ordered in Greek food. Sophie shrugged when her mom placed the order on the phone. The gyro, good though it was, did not take the place of talking to Tony.

Jessica stopped working to check out a shelf full of blue-and-white plates, and to give her dusting arm a chance to rest. As she reached for the feather duster again, Sheriff Valeska walked into Great Finds and said, "April, can I speak with you alone?"

"Sure. Why don't you girls go outside and get a little fresh air?"

Sophie nudged Jessica. "See, I told you, Cousin. We're really big on fresh air here."

Both girls laughed as they went out the door. Jessica stopped to see the posters of exotic places in the window of the travel agency next door. Sophie grabbed her by the arm and pulled her back in front of Great Finds.

"Look," she said to Jessica.

"What?"

"They're talking." Sophie pointed at her mother and the sheriff.

"They're supposed to be talking. This mountain air is shrinking your brain."

"Yeah, but Mom seems concerned. Sheriff Valeska is using the phone. Now Mom's waving us in."

Back inside, Sophie's mom said, "Girls, Sheriff Valeska came to me first to make sure Lucas and I wouldn't mind what was about to happen. I said we would cooperate."

Jessica said, "Cooperate with what?"

Just then, a man in a perfectly fitting gray suit with a crisp white shirt and navy tie walked into the shop. Jessica stared at him. He seemed familiar.

"It's him," she called out and ran over to the sheriff.

"Who?" Sophie asked, staring at the man in front of her. "It *is* him."

14

A Good Guy

Sophie stepped forward. The sheriff may be here, but criminals wouldn't hide behind the law when she was around. "Who are you, really?"

"What's going on, girls?" Sheriff Valeska asked.

"I think I should explain," the man said to them. "Girls, I'm Agent Dallas from the FBI. I had a description of the two girls who had found the briefcase, so I knew who you were when I saw you at the resort. I decided to find out what you knew and warn you to be careful." He looked up at the adults. "They misunderstood and ran away. I hurried after them to explain, but they disappeared."

"We knew you were chasing us, but we also thought the man in the brown suit was after us," Jessica said.

"What man in a brown suit?" he asked.

"The one we've seen over and over again since we found the briefcase."

Agent Dallas pulled a notebook out of his pocket. "Describe him in as much detail as possible. Try not to forget any details no matter how small."

As Jessica did as he'd asked, Sophie studied the FBI agent, trying to learn about his character from his clothes and, more important, the way he moved. Mystery movies and books often said that the way a person stood and gestured showed how he really felt. Nice suit, pretty tie. He stood straight and still like a soldier. When Sophie looked at his feet, she found the shiniest shoes she'd ever seen. She could probably see herself in them.

Jessica stopped talking, so Agent Dallas turned to Sophie. "Anything you would like to add?" He held his pen over his pad.

"Not right now." Turning to Sheriff Valeska, she asked, "Did he show you his ID?"

"Sophie!" her mother exclaimed.

The agent pulled his identification out of his suit pocket and handed it to her. "That is an excellent question."

The ID showed a photo of the man, one that made him appear slightly more dangerous. His perfectly arranged features seemed tougher. Maybe the FBI wanted their agents to look tough in photos. In person, his eyes were a little bluer and his hair a darker shade of brown.

He started to put it away but Jessica stopped him. "Can I see it?"

"Certainly." He handed it to her.

Jessica held up the ID, glancing from it to Agent Dallas. "It sure looks like you."

"It does seem to be official," Sophie said as Jessica handed it back to him. "We'll trust you, since Sheriff Valeska is vouching for you."

"Sophie!" her mother admonished her again.

"The identification is genuine." The agent slipped it back into his coat. "Can you tell me more now?"

In her mind's eye, Sophie could see the man running away from them with the briefcase. "Well . . . he's tough looking. His hair is dark brown or black and kind of wild. And he always wears a brown suit. It's like he doesn't have any other clothes."

"But his suit isn't as nice as yours," Jessica added. "And his shoes were cheap. I know fashion."

"Thank you. Now that we have that out of the way, I need to ask you more questions."

Mrs. Sandoval said, "If this is going to take a while, we could go somewhere where we can sit down. Maybe the deli?"

Agent Dallas said, "I prefer this location. I'd like to keep this situation quiet for now."

"What is 'this situation'? I need to know so that I can protect my daughter and niece."

"We aren't sure. But strange things are happening in Pine Hill."

"You can say that again," Jessica said.

Sheriff Valeska stepped over to the two stools that usually stayed beside the cash register, sat on one, and took a small notebook and pen out of her pocket. Sophie knew they'd told her everything before. Maybe she wanted to be exacting in front of the FBI agent.

Agent Dallas spoke. "Girls, from the beginning, tell me about finding the briefcase."

Sophie told him everything that had happened. When she forgot something, Jessica added it.

"Don't forget about us being followed," Jessica said.

"Followed!" Mrs. Sandoval practically shouted. "You never said anything about that."

"We were never sure. We just had that crawly feeling you get when someone is watching you," Sophie said.

"And a branch broke when we were in the forest." Jessica shuddered.

Sophie said, "And on the trail, we heard crunching on the gravel behind us."

Mrs. Sandoval groaned and sat on the stool next to the sheriff.

"Go on," Agent Dallas said. "Describe what happened at the resort. I ran after you to tell you not to worry, but you had vanished."

Sophie jumped in. "We thought we'd seen the man in the brown suit there earlier—" She looked up at the agent. "We forgot to mention that. Anyway, we didn't know who you were, and you chased us through the resort."

"How did you get away?" he asked.

"There's a hidden tunnel behind the waterfall."

"Well, that is about it." He closed his notebook. "I'm still not sure if the papers you found are anything other than trash, but I would like a copy of them."

Sheriff Valeska stood. "I asked the girls to bring them in today so I could copy them."

"Here." Sophie pulled the papers out of her pocket. Her mother offered the use of her copier, so the sheriff took them and went into the back room.

Agent Dallas put his notebook in his coat pocket. "You've been a great help, girls. Either I or my partner, Agent Able, who is arriving in town tomorrow, will be in touch with you if we have any more questions. I'll leave my card in case you think of something you want to add." He handed it to Sophie. Then as soon as the sheriff returned with the copies, he took the originals and gave the girls and the sheriff copies before leaving.

"Wow," Sophie said.

"Wow is right, Soph." Mrs. Sandoval checked her watch. "It certainly was an action-filled day. We need to close and get home. Your father is going to be getting hungry. I've got some hot dogs in the fridge, so we'll have a quick dinner. Will one of you girls go across the street to the deli and get two pounds of potato salad?" She pulled some money out of her wallet.

"Great." Jessica grinned, put out her hand for the money, and after taking it, hurried out the door.

"Why don't we run over to Bananas and get dessert?" Sophie asked hopefully.

Laughing, Mrs. Sandoval took out more cash, then paused as she was about to hand it to Sophie. "Nothing coated with sugar. But maybe I should call first and tell her what I want."

"Trust me, Mom."

"Don't let me down. You'd better hurry if you want to catch up with your cousin." She handed Sophie the money.

When Sophie walked into the deli, Tony was setting the container of potato salad on the counter. She waited by the door.

"Thanks, Tony." Jessica picked up the container and smiled the whole way to the door.

"Mom wants us to get dessert at Bananas and hurry back." Sophie walked as fast as she could, and Jessica stayed beside her.

"Yum," Jessica said when they went into the bakery.

Mrs. Bowman was on the phone when they walked in. "A down comforter?" she said into the phone.

Sophie and Jessica stopped in their tracks and turned to each other.

The older woman glanced up at them. "I have to go," she said. "Yes, I'll talk to you later."

"Down?" Jessica whispered.

The woman hung up the phone, then asked in what Sophie thought was a nervous voice, "Are you here for a sweet treat?"

Sophie gulped. Were they looking at a thief? She shuffled her feet. "Sorry to interrupt, Mrs. Bowman." Waving Jessica over, she said, "Help me choose something."

Jessica had a panicky expression on her face. Sophie worried she'd freeze up again, but when she looked in the glass bakery cases, the distraction of it helped. She sounded normal when she said, "There's so much to choose from."

"Remember, Mom said 'low sugar.'"

Mrs. Bowman reached into one of the cases and pulled out a cheesecake. "This one isn't too high on the sugar."

Sophie leaned forward to see it better.

"Chocolate swirl banana cheesecake."

Jessica said, "Yum. My mouth is watering."

Sophie agreed, and the older woman packed it up for them.

When they were outside again, Jessica asked, "Do you think she's involved with the criminals?"

Sophie shrugged. "I just don't know. We'd better keep an eye on her."

They were almost back to Great Finds when Sophie said, "The sheriff and FBI agent don't seem sure that the papers we found are important. We've already used them to find clues. I wonder why they can't see that they're valuable?"

"They don't appear important at first. We've done enough work with them to know they are."

"Too true," Sophie said.

On the way home, in the car, Mrs. Sandoval had a bag with some paperwork beside her on the seat, so the two girls sat in the back. Jessica put her hand on the yellow box sitting between them. "That looked so good."

"I know I should have asked you girls earlier, but what's in there?"

"Cheesecake." Sophie held up her hand to stop any protests. "Mrs. Bowman said it was low in sugar. She said it wasn't low in calories, but our family wasn't dieting."

They all laughed.

When Jessica took a bite of her dessert, she said. "This is the best cheesecake. Ever."

Sophie nodded in agreement. "I know. It's strange how all these banana things taste good. And you don't really notice there's banana in most of them."

"What is it with the owner and bananas?"

"No one knows." Mrs. Sandoval added cream to a cup of coffee. "The whole town just figures that she loves them."

"Are you sure you don't want some, Mom?"

She sat down, hesitated for a few seconds, then put a thin slice of the cheesecake on a plate and took a bite. "You're right. This is delicious." She took another bite, then said, "I called the sheriff when you were at the deli and bakery. She said that things seem quiet and safe, so if you promise to stay around people and not wander off without telling me"—she gave Sophie a firm glance—"I think you should take a day off from the mystery and go to the beach again tomorrow."

"Good idea." Sophie gave a thumbs-up to Jessica.

"Yesss! Beach, here we come."

Sophie glanced around at the woods lining the road as they walked to the lake. "You know, Jessica, after all that's happened, I wonder if anyone *is* watching us."

"Good question," Jessica agreed as she scanned the area. "There isn't a car or a person in sight. It's pretty deserted here right now. Let's move faster until we get to people." Jessica started running, so Sophie ran after her, pouring on the speed to pass her a minute later. This time it wasn't quite as easy to get ahead of her cousin.

At Main Street, Sophie stopped, then bent over with her hands on her legs. Panting, she said, "I'll be glad when the FBI and the sheriff arrest the bad guys."

"No kidding." Jessica panted beside her.

"You check really carefully this way," Sophie pointed in the direction of Great Finds, "and I'll check back where we came from. See anything?"

"Nothing suspicious this way."

"Nothing suspicious this way, either." Sophie bent over and got into a racing start position. "Let's go to the beach."

Five minutes later, they'd arrived, peeled off their outer clothes, and were lying on their towels on the beach. The sun felt warm on Sophie's face. "I had to work a little to pass you today."

"Uh-huh. Better watch out."

A cool shadow fell across Sophie, so she opened one eye to look at the cause of it. Agent Dallas towered over them, wearing a suit and dress shoes on the beach. If he'd trailed them here, he must need something from them.

15

Search and Find

Sophie nudged Jessica.

"Huh?" She blinked and looked up. "Oh. It's you."

Agent Dallas smiled. Sophie hadn't been sure that FBI agents were allowed to smile. They never did in movies.

He knelt down. "Can you girls take me to the place you found the briefcase? I've got a team that needs to go through the woods there."

Jessica shrugged. "We've already searched."

"These are professionals. They might find something you missed."

Sophie and Jessica got up, repacked their bags, and slipped their clothes on. "At least I've got the right shoes for it." Jessica pointed at her feet.

Sophie giggled. "Better than the first time."

"Whew. Much better."

The agent watched them curiously. "Follow me to my car."

"Car? It's just a short walk to the trail," Sophie said.

"Even if that's the case, I wouldn't want to leave my car here."

"Leave it at my house. We can walk from there."

At Sophie's house, Agent Dallas took off his suit coat and tie, traded his shoes for hiking boots, and carefully locked all the car doors, pulling on a door handle to check it after he'd closed the door. Obviously from the city. Not many cars were stolen in this small town.

More than one person had told Sophie that Cutoff Trail was difficult for visitors who weren't fit. She looked the agent over. He wasn't overweight and seemed reasonably healthy. He should be fine.

He took off at a fast pace. He wasn't as fit as he appeared to be, though, because ten minutes later he was breathing hard. "Is it much farther?" he asked between breaths.

"It's at the top of the hill and around the bend." Sophie wondered about him. Even Jessica had done better than this—and in flimsy sandals. To be fair, though, Agent Dallas was moving quickly, and Jessica had taken her time that first day.

When they'd walked for a few minutes more, Sophie could hear people talking.

The agent said, "The team must have been able to follow the map Sheriff Valeska gave them." He seemed relieved.

Sophie grinned. She wasn't sure if he was happier to find everyone here or happier to be able to stop walking uphill.

He straightened his shoulders and got his in-charge, FBI look back. "Show us exactly where you found the briefcase."

Jessica walked over and tapped her foot on the spot. "Here."

"We won't need anything more from you girls. Would you like one of my agents to escort you home?"

Jessica and Sophie glanced at each other.

"I want to watch," Sophie said.

"Me too," Jessica agreed.

"Then stay out of the way."

The FBI team made a circle from the briefcase's location out. A dozen people searched behind every bush and under every rock. Some of them moved out of view down the path.

"They *are* searching more carefully than we did," Jessica said.

"That's because they're getting paid to do it."

Jessica giggled.

Just then, an agent walked up to Agent Dallas. Sophie could barely hear her low voice telling him they'd found something. She watched as Agent Dallas followed the woman down the path, around the corner, and out of sight.

"I'd love to see their clue."

"Why don't we casually walk down the path?" Jessica started walking slowly, whistling as she went and looking around.

All the agents stopped what they were doing to watch her.

Sophie laughed so hard that she couldn't move. "Jessica, wait," she choked out when she could and hurried to catch up with her. "Instead of whistling, maybe you should scream at the top of your lungs."

"Huh?"

"You made so much noise that everyone stopped working so they could see what you were doing."

When Jessica paused and saw all the agents watching her, her face turned bright red. "How embarrassing. They do that in the movies and everyone ignores them. Shows you how real movies are."

Sophie spotted the agent by the nail-polish rock. "Hey, look!" Sophie pointed to her. "She and Agent Dallas have knelt next to the rock we turned over."

The girls walked up to the agents and overheard the woman say, "Nail polish wouldn't normally be here, and it being hidden by flipping the rock could make this important."

Sophie and Jessica giggled.

"Can I help you girls?" Agent Dallas asked with an annoyed tone.

Sophie said, "Actually, I think I can help you."

"How would you do that? We have an important clue here that you girls overlooked. I told you professionals could find things you had missed."

Sophie resisted the urge to roll her eyes. Jessica reached out her hand and held it next to the polish on the rock.

The agent looked from Jessica's nails to the rock and back again.

"Did you do this on purpose?" Agent Dallas gave them a look that Sophie figured had made grown men cringe in fear.

"No. I dropped the bottle of polish. We turned the rock over because we didn't want to leave a mess."

The other agent set the rock back down and glared at them. She definitely wasn't happy that her evidence was really just part of a bungled manicure.

Jessica nudged Sophie and gestured uphill with her thumb. Sophie headed up the hill after her. Agent Dallas might ask them to leave if they stayed there any longer.

From the top they watched the proceedings. Sophie cocked her head to the side. "You know, I forgot to search over the side of the hill."

"That isn't a hill. It's a cliff. It goes straight down." Jessica rubbed her arms like a chill had gone through her.

"Actually, it just looks like that from here. There are lots of ledges. You can climb down from ledge to ledge."

"Really?" Jessica approached the edge but stopped a few feet from it.

Sophie walked over to it, lay down, and scooted on her stomach to peer over the edge. Still facing down, she waved Jessica over. "Look!"

Jessica lay down next to Sophie and slowly scooted toward the edge. "It's a suitcase!"

"Do you think Agent Dallas is going to like it if two girls find him a clue?"

"Not a bit."

"Maybe we should make the guy look good."

Jessica slowly grinned. "What did you have in mind?"

"Let's talk about the hill over by him. Maybe he will overhear us and do something about it."

"It's worth a try."

They found him near the nail-polish rock. People still combed the woods for clues. A few feet from him, she and Jessica paused and turned toward each other. Sophie winked.

"You know Jessica, something might be over the side of the hill," Sophie said loudly.

"But that's a cliff, Sophie. Anything that fell over would be in the lake at the bottom."

"No, it only seems like a cliff to strangers to Pine Hill. You can climb down it fairly easily."

Agent Dallas froze. They had his attention now.

The girls walked back near the edge and sat on a boulder to see what happened.

Jessica could hear Agent Dallas shout at one of his team members. "Hey, Morgan, go check over the side of the hill." He pointed in their direction.

"The hill?" The man turned where his boss pointed. "You mean the cliff? Maybe we should bring a boat around the lake to inspect the base of it."

"Just do me a favor and check over the hill."

The man shrugged. "Sure."

He and Agent Dallas walked to the top of the hill then slowly edged forward to peer over.

"Look!" Morgan pointed down the cliff.

Jessica smiled at Sophie. "Your word exactly."

"I'm a genius with language."

Jessica laughed.

Morgan scooted backward over the cliff and came back with a large, blue suitcase.

Sophie kept her eyes on the suitcase until Morgan carried it out of sight. "I'll bet there are a lot of clues in a suitcase that size. I wonder if they'll let us see what's inside."

The girls moved close enough to the agents to hear that it would be opened back at the lab.

Agent Dallas motioned them over. "Thank you."

"For what?" Sophie looked at him innocently.

"You know. I appreciate your help." He walked away.

"Our work is done here," Sophie said. She'd helped the FBI. If only she could tell someone about everything that had happened.

Back at the house, Jessica knew something different was up when Sophie went into the kitchen, opened the fridge, and pulled out chicken and vegetables.

"I would ask if you're making a snack, but it would be a strange snack."

"I haven't made dinner in a while, and it might make Mom and Dad happy if I do. They seemed a bit overwhelmed by the idea of us working with an FBI agent."

"Working with the FBI is a bit of an exaggeration. He asked us questions. Will your parents be happy eating something you cook?"

"I can cook. Mom taught me how when I was little." After grabbing a large pan, Sophie next moved everything to a cutting board. "How does a chicken stir-fry and fruit salad sound?"

"Great. Can I help?"

"Sure. Get out a big bowl for the fruit salad. Then cut up whatever fruit is ripe, making enough for the four of us."

Jessica carefully cut up a couple of peaches, a plum, and some cherries.

Sophie put rice on to cook, then cut up the chicken and veggies. "I saw blueberries in the fridge. Throw some of those in there. And pour a little orange juice over it so the fruit doesn't turn brown."

A few minutes later, Jessica stood back and admired her work. "I did it. I made a fruit salad. Anything else?"

"It's good as is. You could add some honey and cinnamon to yogurt and make a sauce. Then it's more of a dessert."

Jessica grinned. "I'm on it." She got out the three ingredients, combined them, and tasted as she went. "This is great. I'll make this when I get home." She didn't think her mom would be too happy if she made a whole dinner because of the possible scary results, but Sophie's parents were happy and appeared relaxed when Sophie told them about their day.

Uncle Lucas leaned back in his chair and listened as Sophie described how she'd found the suitcase. Shaking his head in amazement, he spooned some fruit into a bowl. "If the FBI want you to go back there with them, I'll take time off work and tag along."

"Is business okay, Dad? To be able to take time off in the middle of the day?"

"It's fine. I did meet a man the other day who asked me about buying my business."

Jessica said, "Just like Aunt April."

"Not quite. Your aunt and I own the building Great Finds is in, and if she sold the business, she would also sell her inventory—all of the antiques in the store. Her business is worth a lot to anyone. My business is different. It's based on my brains, and my office is a room in our house, so without me, it isn't worth much. The offer doesn't make sense."

"That's another strange thing that I'll have to think about." Sophie slowly put a bite of fruit into her mouth.

Her dad rolled his eyes. "Our little crime fighter. Right, April?"

Her mother sighed. "Yes."

After dinner Jessica sat down in an old, comfy chair, and Sophie settled onto the couch while her mom and dad cleaned up in the kitchen—their thank-you for dinner. Sophie almost immediately sprang to her feet and began pacing back and forth across the room.

"Sophie, stop!" Jessica closed her eyes and tried to ignore her. That proved to be impossible when Sophie kept going. "Not one more lap across the room! Please."

"I want to *do* something. I need to get out into the fresh air. Maybe go camping or something like that. I know Mom and Dad *won't* let me do that right now." Sophie perked up. "Hey, maybe we could sit outside tonight. Talk about the mystery. That might be the closest I come to camping under the stars until this is solved."

Jessica didn't want to sit outside, but Sophie seemed so sad about not being able to go camping, something Jessica wanted to do even less, that she agreed. "Okay." How bad could it be?

"Great. I'll make some snacks."

An hour later Jessica brushed a couple of mosquitoes off her arm, two of what seemed like thousands that were trying to eat her alive. "Pass me the popcorn." When Sophie did, she tossed some into her mouth. "I wish mosquitoes ate this instead of me."

"Sitting out here in the dark makes me think about the guy who dropped his briefcase in the night and ran. Why would someone do that?"

Something swooped above Jessica, diving close to her head. She dropped forward onto her knees, popcorn flying into the air. "What was that?"

Sophie stood next to her and chewed on her lip. "Don't worry. It wouldn't hurt you."

Jessica glared at her. "I know you aren't telling me something. What was it? It didn't seem to be a bird. Besides, it's dark and I don't think birds fly at night. I remember you told me bats and owls flew at night. An owl?"

Sophie scuffed the ground with the toe of her shoe. "A bat."

"Did you say a *bat*?"

"Uh, yeah."

"I'm out of here." Jessica ran for the back door. "The bat can have my popcorn."

Sophie chased after her cousin. "Bats don't hurt you."

Jessica stood inside the open back door. "Are you sure?"

"Uh-huh. I'm pretty sure they don't eat popcorn either."

Jessica paused to think about it. "I'm sorry, but I think I've had enough of the outdoors for tonight." When she started to walk away, she stopped. "I also think that bat answers loud and clear why anyone would get scared in the woods at night and abandon their luggage."

When Sophie came into the bedroom an hour later, she told Jessica about the possum with its babies she'd seen. But even cute possums couldn't make up for bats.

16

Clues in the News

On the way to the newspaper office, Jessica and Sophie decided they had no choice but to tell Mr. Avinson about the two pieces of newspaper they'd found. After explaining, they showed them to him.

"Hmm. It can't be." He held the piece of an article close to the light, carefully examining it.

"What can't be?" Sophie asked, moving closer to the light.

"The style of type—that's the way the letters look—is the same. The page's layout is the same." Mr. Avinson turned to them. "I believe these are corners of articles from the *Pine Hill Press*. I have a computer list of all the articles going back fifty years. We can search it for some of the words we see here." He sat at his computer and started typing. "The word 'Down' is at the edge of one of the pieces of newspaper, with the rest of the sentence torn away, and it's capitalized," he said as he typed.

"What?" Sophie exclaimed.

Both girls crowded closer to read the computer screen.

"Why didn't we notice that?"

"Only one subject matches it: Down Shoppe."

Sophie and Jessica stared at each other, then Sophie said, "It's a new business over on Olympic Street, but it hasn't opened yet."

"Hmm. Three articles." Mr. Avinson's forehead furrowed. "I know we wrote something about it, but that's too many articles for a business that hasn't opened." He paged through the list. "I can read summaries of the articles here. Yes. This explains why. There was a Down Shoppe seven years ago, and two of the articles are about the earlier business."

He put his elbow on the table and rested his chin on his fist. "That was before I bought the newspaper, so I don't remember those articles. I do remember the fishing store that was there last year, but I guess they closed permanently. Let's print a list of these dates and get the papers for you." He hit Print and picked up the pages that slid out of his printer.

Taking them, he walked over to shelves lining the wall that were stacked high with newspapers and pulled three out, one by one. "Come on over and sit down." He set the newspapers on a table and added his printout to the pile. "This sheet shows which article is on which page. I have to finish an article for the newspaper, so I'll let you ladies work on this." He walked back to his desk and sat in front of a computer.

Jessica went through the list. "I can read the old articles, Sophie, and you can read the new one. How's that?"

"As long as my one article is twice as interesting as yours, that's okay." Sophie laughed.

Jessica handed the newer paper to Sophie and picked up the printout. "Your article is on page 2." Jessica found her articles on the list and turned to them. As soon as she saw the first one, she felt like jumping up and down and shouting. Excited, she studied the photo that went with it and read the entire article. Then she reached for the second newspaper, hoping to find something just as good.

When she finished hers, she saw that Sophie had finished too. "Look at this!" Jessica held up the first newspaper she'd read. "This article matches the corner of the one we found." She held the actual newspaper next to their corner of newspaper.

"Score!"

"There's more—the new Down Shoppe looks just like the old one in the photo."

Mr. Avinson walked over to the girls and bent over them to see the photo. Shaking his head, he said, "This certainly is odd. I haven't been on Olympic Street in a couple of weeks, so I haven't seen the new Down Shoppe sign. Maybe we made a mistake and used an old photo for the new story."

"Uh-uh." Sophie shook her head. "We walked by there a few days ago, and it's exactly like this photo. Maybe the same people started both businesses."

"It doesn't seem likely," Jessica commented. "My second article mentioned that the earlier business never opened because the owners suddenly decided to move to Italy."

Sophie leaned back in her chair. "Mine didn't say much about the new shop. Maybe the reporter didn't find many facts."

Mr. Avinson said, "That's an interesting observation. I remember her saying that she had to ask around to try and find information for the article because she couldn't get ahold of the owners."

"Why did you publish the article, then?" Jessica asked.

He chuckled. "Sophie, I think you can tell her."

Sophie smiled back. "Because anything new in town is news. Right?"

"Right."

Sophie snapped her fingers. "My article said that the new owners hadn't been to Pine Hill until a month ago. How can the two businesses look the same?"

Mr. Avinson furrowed his brow. "Everything about this is unusual. I believe we should explain the situation to Sheriff Valeska."

"Agreed," Jessica and Sophie said in unison.

"Are you sure you've only been together for a week or two?"

They nodded excitedly.

"We have a clue," Sophie called out and waved the newspapers in the air as they entered the sheriff's office.

Sheriff Valeska put her head on her desk. "No more!"

"This is a fascinating development," Mr. Avinson said.

The sheriff lifted her head. "I didn't see you behind the girls, Frank. Is there really a clue?"

The three told her what they'd found. As they stood there, the phone rang.

The sheriff answered, listened a moment, then said, "Yes, April. I'll make a note of it." She hung up.

"Did my mom call to check on us?"

"No. A woman offered to buy Great Finds."

"That's strange. First Mom, then Dad, now Mom again. Jessica, let's run by Great Finds and ask her about it." Sophie said good-bye to Mr. Avinson and the sheriff, then ran over to her mom's shop.

Once there, Sophie grilled her mother. "Can you describe her?"

"She'd be hard to forget with a bright flowered dress and matching hat. It was a bit much for downtown Pine Hill."

"She sounds like someone we've seen before." Sophie then told her mother about what they'd learned at the newspaper.

"You girls stay out of trouble."

"Of course," Sophie answered.

"I hope trouble stays away from us," Jessica added quietly.

Sophie led Jessica to the back of the shop. When they sat down, Sophie on the floor, Jessica on the stool, Sophie said, "We need to know a lot more about down. I know that Mom and Dad have a down comforter on their bed."

"So?"

"So, maybe we can carefully open it and see if what's inside is the same as what we found in the briefcase."

"Oh, Sophie! If your parents found out—"

"I know. But we have to solve this mystery."

There must be a way to go about it that wouldn't get them in what Jessica knew would be big trouble.

"Well?" Sophie asked.

A solution came to mind. "It might help if we knew more about what was going on in town when the other

Down Shoppe was here. Maybe we could look through more newspapers."

"Let's call Mr. Avinson." Sophie ran to the phone, and soon received an answer that had her smiling. "He says we can go back there right now. If it's okay with Mom, he's going to leave the key with us so he can go to a meeting and we can lock up when we're done."

Her mother agreed. "It's fine with me as long as you're back here by about four o'clock. I'm thinking of closing early today."

The girls hurried to the deli—Tony wasn't there—and picked up some sandwiches and chips to go before heading over to the newspaper.

When they arrived, Mr. Avinson said, "I certainly enjoyed our research earlier."

Sophie said, "We did too. Thank you for letting us come back."

He took them back to the same table. "In case you girls didn't notice where I was getting the newspapers for our research, this area is for the year when the other Down Shoppe existed, and"—he stepped a few feet to his right—"here are the recent issues. If you're comfortable working alone on your project, I'm going to my meeting."

"No problem," Sophie said.

As he gathered up his things to take, including a briefcase, Jessica asked, "How do you become a newspaper reporter?" Images of working in exotic places, writing about important stories, excited her.

"Most people study journalism in college. I did. Is newswriting something you're interested in?

Jessica glanced over at the stacks of newspapers. "Maybe. I know I enjoy writing, but I've never written a newspaper article."

"If you'd like to write one, I'll read it. If I like it, I'll publish it in the paper."

"Thank you. I'll keep my eyes open for exciting ideas. You know—"

Sophie interrupted her. "Give it time, Jessica. You can bounce ideas off me."

Yikes. She'd almost spilled the story. And to a newspaperman.

"Here's a key." Mr. Avinson set it on his desk. "It fits both the back and front doors, but the front door lock can be a little fussy, so I'll lock it now. Go out the back door and drop the key through the front mail slot." He locked the front lock from the inside, jiggling the knob a bit as he did so.

When he went toward the back door, Jessica called out, "Thank you again, Mr. Avinson."

"Yes, thanks." Sophie added.

He waved as he pulled the door closed.

As soon as it closed completely, Sophie said, "Jessica, you were going to tell him about our mystery. He knows some of what's happened, but not most of it."

"Sorry. All of the recent activity on the mystery is so exciting that it immediately came to mind."

"Maybe you can write the story about our mystery after we solve it."

"I've been thinking about doing that." Jessica spotted the bag from the deli and realized she was hungry. "But let's eat before we work." As she unwrapped her sandwich, she asked, "How far back before the articles do you think we should read?"

Sophie tore open her bag of chips. "I've been thinking about that. How about a month before, and for the older ones, a month after?"

"Sounds good to me."

After eating, they washed their hands and got to work.

"I'll get the earlier ones." Jessica sorted through the newspapers and pulled four of them off the shelf. "I'm quite happy the *Pine Hill Press* only comes out once a week."

Sophie walked over to the later newspapers and pulled off a stack. Both girls set their papers down and read in silence for a while. When Jessica reached for the second to last newspaper, she said, "I'm almost through the time when the other shop was there."

Sophie kept reading and muttered, "Uh-huh." Then she stretched and asked, "Have you found anything interesting?"

Jessica flipped the page. "Not until now. Sophie . . ."

Sophie sat up. "What'd you find?"

"On the other side of the article about the first Down Shoppe, the one we found in the alley, there's an article about all of the money residents make off visitors each summer. The idea of a lot of money might bring in criminals. Pine Hill was called the 'richest little city in the state.'"

"I remember learning about that in school." Sophie rested her elbows on the table. "Other newspapers printed the articles. After that, people flooded into town trying to buy up land for the boom they expected to happen. But I don't think it ever did. Does it say that?"

"No. At the end of the article, it says to see the next issue for the conclusion." Jessica picked up the last newspaper. "It was front-page news in the next newspaper. The town went wild with people wanting to make a fortune off visitors to the city."

Sophie laughed. "I doubt that's an article we need. We'd better keep reading."

The phone rang a couple of times, but they didn't think they should pick it up.

When Jessica finished the little reading she had left, she rubbed her eyes. "No more newspapers, please. I don't even want to see one for a while."

Sophie closed her eyes and rolled her shoulders. Looking up, she said, "We haven't found anything that seems important. But maybe we've missed something."

Jessica felt the same way. "If we have, maybe we'll know later. There might be a piece of the puzzle we won't know is important until we have the rest of the pieces fitted together."

Sophie gathered the newspapers together. Then she checked the time. "Jessica, it's after four. We're late, and I don't think Mom will be happy."

"Understatement of the century." Jessica returned the papers to the shelf in the order they'd found them. "I want to make sure we leave things as we found them."

"Me too. It was really nice of Mr. Avinson to let us stay here without him."

Sophie turned off the lights, and Jessica went out the door first. While Sophie locked it, Jessica stood behind her in the alley. Something moved to her right.

Jessica gulped, slowly turned to the right and saw . . .
a stack of empty boxes waiting for trash pickup. She let
out a deep breath. "I'm getting jumpy."

"Why do you say that?"

"I thought I saw something move, but when I turned
that way, all I saw was garbage."

Sophie looked around the shadowy alley and shivered.
"Maybe the flap on a box moved in the breeze. Let's get
back on Main Street."

They dropped the key through the mail slot, then hurried to Great Finds.

Once there, Sophie opened the door and put on a big
smile. "Hi, Mom."

Her mother pushed some paperwork to the side, an
angry expression on her face. "Why are you late?"

"Well—"

She held up her hand to stop her. "I was worried about
you. I called the newspaper office and no one answered."

"We didn't think we should answer the phone there."

Her mother glared at her, picked up her purse, and
ushered them out of the building.

As they walked to her car, Jessica couldn't think of anything to say. The normally short drive seemed to take
forever. When Aunt April pulled up in front of their house,
Jessica hurried out the car door and rushed inside.

When she and Sophie got to the bedroom, Sophie
quickly closed the door. "Whew, I haven't seen Mom that
mad since I forgot to clean the house and the mayor came
for dinner."

Jessica giggled. "You must have gotten in a lot of trouble."

"That's the truth." Sophie flopped down on her bed. "The good news is that she cools off pretty quickly. Unless she gets Dad involved."

A knock sounded at the door.

"Yes?" Sophie called out.

"It's Dad."

"Uh-oh." Sophie fell backward on her bed. "Come in."

He started talking the second he opened the door. "Sophie Eileen, your mother was worried about you today."

She sat back up. "I know, Dad. We were safe. When we did see we were a little late, we still had to straighten up."

Jessica heard her uncle Lucas sigh. Then he turned to leave. "I'll explain the situation to your mother," he told Sophie. "She'll understand that you were trying to follow the rules."

Sophie turned to Jessica when he closed the door. "Whew. That was better than I expected."

Aunt April didn't seem angry when they sat down to dinner, and by the time they finished, she was smiling. But she didn't bring out any dessert. Not even fruit.

After dinner, Sophie pulled out a pad of paper and a pen, along with the papers they'd found. "Let's list all of our possible clues to see if anything helps."

Jessica could certainly get behind the idea of bringing organization to their efforts. "Why don't we make two columns, one with things we know are clues and the other with things that might be clues."

Sophie nodded. "I like that."

When it came to the newspapers they'd searched through today, Jessica argued against Sophie's take on them. "I don't think we can put the newspapers we read in the clue column. We don't know if they really helped."

"Sure, they did. We know there was an earlier Down Shoppe."

"But we don't know if that means anything."

Sophie argued. "It has to. The new Down Shoppe is a clue."

"Agreed."

"Then the old one has to be, because they look the same. They must be connected."

Jessica sighed. "You win. All those years of reading and watching mysteries did teach you something."

They looked through the legal pages and the newspaper bits one more time, but nothing new stood out.

When Jessica went to bed that night, she picked up one of Sophie's mysteries to read. Maybe she would get some ideas from it.

17

Bad Guy Alert

After breakfast, Sophie got a surprise when Jessica said, "Let's go by the Down Shoppe. Just to see if anything's different."

"I like that. You're starting to think like a detective. Let's case the joint."

"I think that's what criminals say before they check out a place they want to rob."

No other awesome detective sayings came to mind. "Let's go see what's what."

Not far from the Down Shoppe, Sophie noticed a man following them. "Jessica, is that the guy in the brown suit, or am I seeing things?"

Jessica looked in the same direction. "I don't know. He's so far away that I can't even tell what he's wearing. It could be a man in a suit, but he might be wearing jeans and a jacket. It could be anyone, including Uncle Lucas."

"Let's walk faster and see if he follows us."

"Two things: What if that man, whoever he is, already planned to walk this direction? And even if he is the man in the brown suit, he's far enough away that he probably doesn't know who he's following."

They walked a little faster, then a little faster than that.

Sophie looked over her shoulder. "He's wearing navy pants and a tan jacket, and he's going faster than we are. He's gaining on us. Run to the sheriff's office!"

The girls ran the three blocks and plunged through the door.

"Girls, what's wrong?" Sheriff Valeska hurried over to them.

"Man," Jessica panted, "chasing us."

The sheriff pushed open the door and surveyed the area. "I don't see anyone."

Sophie checked. "He's gone. But you've got to believe us."

"I do." Sheriff Valeska pointed to the chairs. "Sit, ladies, and rest. We received the results on the fingerprints in the briefcase a few minutes ago. Now I see why the FBI was so interested. They must have suspected something like this."

"Like what?" Jessica bent forward in the chair, still panting.

"The fingerprints belong to a serious bad guy. You must stay in public and together. And if you see anything suspicious, call immediately." Sheriff Valeska sat behind her desk. "Do you understand, girls?"

Jessica took a big breath. "I sure do."

The sheriff leaned toward Sophie. "Listen carefully to me. Do not wait. Do not investigate. Call."

"We understand," Sophie said. The excitement of having a real mystery with a real criminal slipped away from her.

"It's best this way, Sophie."

"I know, but it isn't as exciting. For a little while, it was like living in a detective book or movie."

The sheriff grabbed her hat and headed for the door. "I'd planned to call your mom today to tell her about the fingerprints. Since you're here, I'll walk you over there. Would you like to listen in?"

"Yes. Thanks." Sophie felt like smiling again.

A few minutes later, Sheriff Valeska explained to her mother, "We've received the fingerprint report. The man whose fingerprints were in the briefcase is a known criminal. He's someone the FBI has been after for several years."

Mrs. Sandoval gasped.

"I know you've been watching the girls carefully, but I want you to fully understand what's going on. We don't want them vulnerable to strange men, like earlier today."

"Earlier?"

"That's right. You couldn't know yet. A man chased them into town. Keep them in public and together." The sheriff walked over to the door.

"I'll keep them here during the day."

Sophie's summer crumbled to the ground. "Oh, Mom."

"You're safe here, Soph," Mrs. Sandoval said.

The sheriff agreed. "Yes, this should all be over in a few days," she said as she left.

"Jessica, I've got a good news, bad news scenario," Mrs. Sandoval said.

"You're going to call my mom and dad, aren't you?"

"I don't want them to worry, but I can't keep something like this from them. I'll call tonight."

"Great. I haven't talked to them for a few days." Jessica didn't seem worried about the call.

The bell at the front door rang as Agent Dallas came into Great Finds. He started speaking as the door closed behind him. "Sheriff Valeska told me what happened this morning. Are you girls all right?"

"They're fine," Mrs. Sandoval said. "Will you solve this soon?"

The agent grimaced. "We get one clue that leads nowhere. Then we get another one . . ."

Sophie said, "That's exactly what happened to us. We wrote down everything we knew about the case last night and studied the papers. But we didn't notice anything new. What clue are you working on now?"

"That's right," he said slowly. "We're working on the original papers in our lab. But you still have copies. I'll come by tonight to get them. You aren't safe as long as you have any evidence that might be associated with this case."

Jessica asked, "If the bad guy *thinks* we have them, aren't we in danger even if we don't?"

"I admire your logic, but I don't want you to have anything associated with this crime. I think you'll be safest without them."

Mrs. Sandoval said, "Let's hope the criminals are paying as much attention as you think they are."

When Agent Dallas turned to leave, Sophie said, "Wait. What was in the suitcase?"

He stopped, not moving for a few seconds, then faced them. "Mostly clothing."

"Men's or women's?" Sophie asked.

"I shouldn't tell you anything. But it was both. And that's all I'm saying. Now, I have to be going." The bell signaled his departure.

When her mother went to the back of the store, Sophie said, "That suitcase was a great clue."

"It was filled with clothes, Sophie. How is that a great clue?"

Sophie felt like the mystery was starting to come together. "It shows that there's a man and a woman in this."

"You're absolutely right. Maybe it's the man who just chased us and the pretend French woman."

All of the people they'd seen doing odd things flashed through Sophie's mind, but Jessica's theory was as good as any. "Might be."

After dinner they called Jessica's parents. Sophie could tell from Jessica's answers that her mother was worried.

"No, Mom, everything's fine. I'm safe. The FBI is taking care of us."

Sophie winced when her aunt Stephanie, Jessica's mother, shrieked so loudly she could hear it. Jessica jumped and moved the phone a few inches from her ear. She heard a few more loud things Aunt Stephanie said. Her cousin nodded and said, "Yes, Mom" over and over. Then she held out the phone to her aunt April. "Mom said, 'Put my sister on.'"

After taking the phone, she said, "Yes, Sis. They're fine." Then she listened for a while, not saying anything, before passing the phone back to Jessica.

When Jessica hung up, Mrs. Sandoval said, "Your mother was concerned."

"Tell me about it. She didn't know about the FBI until I told her, and it totally upset her that the situation required major law enforcement, not just the sheriff. Big mistake."

"But it *was* right to tell her."

Later that night, the girls watched one of Sophie's favorite mysteries from her library of movies. As the end credits rolled by, Jessica said, "You know, I'm surprised that Agent Dallas never came to get the papers."

"As much as I didn't want to give them to him, I find it strange too."

18

Catching Clues

"Let's give the FBI a call."

"They aren't going to care about a call from someone our age."

"Let's try." Jessica dialed the phone number on Agent Dallas' card and asked for him, explaining that they had a clue for him.

A minute later, Jessica hung up and sighed. "The woman told me he wasn't available and took a message. She didn't seem to think this was important."

"Told you so."

"They must get a lot of calls from people telling them they have clues, so I doubt that it's because I'm twelve. She can't see through the phone."

"And you don't sound like a little kid."

"Thank you. I tried to sound older."

The whole situation puzzled Jessica. Why hadn't an FBI agent done what he'd said? "Maybe we'll get a call from Agent Dallas tomorrow. He could just be busy with the case."

During church the next morning, Sophie thought about the rest of the day. Staring straight ahead, she said out of the corner of her mouth, "How about a hike?"

Jessica wrinkled her nose. "I don't think so."

"Okay," Sophie said slowly. "Then how about walking down by the lake like last Sunday? It should be fun on a sunny summer Sunday. Ooh, I like how that sounds. Sunny summer Sunday."

"Shh." Her mother put her finger over her mouth and glared at them in a way that made Sophie cringe. Her mom had thankfully refocused on the minister's lesson when a minute or two later Jessica nudged her and gave a thumbs-up.

The whole family ate lunch in a small Mexican restaurant. Then Sophie's parents dropped them off at the lake with directions to stay together and around people. They'd be back to pick them up in a couple of hours.

Sophie hoped they'd be less protective after a while. A man had chased them, but he hadn't caught them. Walking toward the water she said, "Let's go over by the boats."

"Are they far?"

"Nope. Just over to the right."

As they got close to the docks, Jessica said, "There are boats tied up in all colors and sizes. The lake's bigger than I realized."

A big, burly man on a large boat came into view. Sophie said, "Hey, Captain Jack."

"Hello, lassie."

Jessica turned to Sophie. "From Scotland?"

"Yes. He's a friend of Dad's. But how do you know those things?"

"Scotland's attached to England, the country I live in."

Just one more thing that she and Jessica didn't have in common.

As they stepped to the side of the boat, Sophie said to the captain, "I'm surprised to see you at the dock this time of day."

"I'm not booked today and was getting ready to go fishing by myself. You know, I haven't taken you fishing in quite a while." He rubbed his bearded chin. "Would you like a short trip?"

Sophie explained to Jessica, "Captain Jack owns a charter boat. People pay him to take them fishing."

"My uncle Bill does that too," Jessica said, then asked, "Will your parents allow us to go? I can call." She pulled her cell phone out of her purse. "No, I can't."

Captain Jack smiled. "No one's phone works here, so we use the pay phone onshore. Lassie, why don't ye call and ask?"

Sophie raced up to the phone and came back in two minutes. "We can go."

As Captain Jack prepared to leave and the girls waited on the back of the boat, Sophie told Jessica, "Mom was thrilled. She said we'd be safe on the water, where no one could get to us."

Jessica glanced over at the shore. "When you put it like that, being on the boat does sound better than being on land."

Once they were on the lake, Captain Jack slowed the boat to a crawl, reached for two fishing poles, and handed one of them to Sophie. Then he walked over to Jessica.

"I'm not fishing." Jessica crossed her arms in defiance.

Captain Jack stopped in front of her with a pole. "Don't you like fish, lassie?"

"I love fish. On a plate. But I'm not putting a hook through a wiggling worm to catch one."

Captain Jack roared with laughter. "Lassie, I don't want you to miss the fun of fishing." He reached into a cabinet and pulled out a bag of marshmallows. "Would this suit you?"

Jessica eyed him suspiciously. "Are you teasing me?"

"No. The fish love them." He tore open the bag and put one of the marshmallows in his mouth. "Matter of fact, 'tis true that I like them too."

Jessica smiled. "Cousin, let's each catch a big fish."

"Deal," Sophie said and baited her hook with a marshmallow. Jessica copied what she did.

As Captain Jack motored them slowly across the smooth lake, with their lines pulling in the water, Sophie looked around them and up to the sky. Several large birds flew high in the direction of the boat. She shaded her eyes with her hand to watch them.

Captain Jack looked up. "Those ducks are beauties. Have ye become a bird-watcher?"

"No. But we are trying to find the bird that matches a feather we found."

The birds dipped down toward the water, then up over the boat. A couple of feathers fell off of them as they passed overhead.

Excited, Sophie asked, "Can we catch a feather, Captain Jack?"

"There's a breeze today, so I'm not sure where they'll drop. I'll try to maneuver the deck under them, but you lassies need to grab a fishnet each and be ready to scoop them up." Sophie reached for the net beside her, and Jessica rested her pole against the side of the boat so she could grab another.

The captain cut the motor and, staring upward, carefully turned the wheel. At the last minute, the breeze shifted sending one feather into the lake and out of sight. When the other feather fluttered above the water for a second, Jessica scooped it up in her net.

Sophie plucked it out of the net. "Jessica, take a look at this feather. I think it's exactly like ours! And there's some of the fluffy white stuff with it."

"That's a bit of the down from the duck," Captain Jack said.

Sophie blinked, startled. "Down comes with duck feathers?" How had they missed this fact?

"Aye, Lassie. And geese. I'm surprised someone who enjoys the outdoors as much as you doesn't know about our winged friends."

"Me too. I'll be learning more." She pulled on the bit of fluff and muttered, "So down comes *with* duck feathers."

They fished for a while longer but didn't catch anything.

Jessica handed her pole to Captain Jack when they reached the shore. "I'm not sure if I should be sorry I didn't catch anything or glad I didn't have to touch a slimy fish."

He chuckled. "I'll make sure you catch a fish this summer. You and Sophie can come out with me another time."

"Thank you. I think." Jessica smiled at him. "A bat attacked me and I survived, so I guess catching a fish is next. This is a summer of adventure. Thank you for helping us catch the feather."

Sophie held the feather up in the light as they walked back down the pier. "I can't wait to take this over to Sheriff Valeska tomorrow so we can compare it to our old feather."

"Are you sure she isn't there on Sunday? Maybe we should try."

"The office isn't really open. There's just a deputy on call for emergencies."

Sophie called her parents from the phone she'd used earlier, and her dad drove over to pick them up.

Back at home, Jessica stretched out on her bed and put her hands behind her head. "We've had quite a day."

Sophie grinned, "We couldn't ask for more than a piece of the puzzle falling from the sky."

They were in their robes after their morning showers and sitting on their beds talking when someone knocked on the bedroom door. Sophie called, "Come in," and her dad stepped inside.

"Girls, I'm heading out early for a meeting, so I can drop you off at Great Finds. I think you're safe as long as you're together, but you may as well take advantage of the ride."

Sophie answered, "Sounds good to me, and I don't think Jessica will argue."

"Not a chance I'll say no." Knowing they were inside a car, so no one would follow or chase them as they walked to town, was all good.

When her uncle had closed the bedroom door, Jessica headed for the closet. "It's great that you have a dad like that."

"I like your dad too. I haven't seen him in a long time, but I remember he's nice."

"I love my dad. But he's gone a lot, and I don't really know what he does at work. Your dad is here all the time."

"My dad's here all day. But I don't understand accounting. Your dad is gone for months at a time. Are you missing him again?"

Jessica wondered what her mom and dad were doing right now. "I miss my whole family."

"Even Frog Boy?"

Jessica's brother was going out on a boat every day, so he may not have even noticed that she wasn't there. But she still thought about him. "Yes, I even miss him."

On the way to town, Sophie asked her dad to drop them off at the sheriff's office instead of Great Finds.

"Sheriff Valeska," Sophie called out as she opened the door and hurried inside.

"Yes, Sophie." The sheriff sighed.

"We found a feather. Can we hold it next to the one from the briefcase?"

The sheriff hesitated, then said, "Why not?" She disappeared into the back, then returned a few minutes later with the feather in a labeled plastic bag.

The girls held theirs next to it and smiled.

"It's a match," Sheriff Valeska said in amazement.

"It's from a duck. Captain Jack knows which kind."

"Thanks. The waterfowl biologist is on vacation, so the feather hasn't been identified."

Huh. The sheriff had to call Fish and Game too.

At Great Finds Jessica set her purse down on a back shelf and picked up the duster—her job. Again. Glass shelves seemed to attract dust.

"Girls, I usually put out a Be Right Back sign in the window when I need to run an errand, but since you're here . . ." Her aunt's words trailed off and she stared at them.

"Mom, we can handle things for a few minutes."

"Okay, Soph. If a customer wants to buy something, you know what to do. If they have a question you can't answer, get their phone number, and I can call them as soon as I get back."

"Sure." Sophie smiled sweetly.

"I'll only be gone about forty-five minutes," Mrs. Sandoval said as she walked out the door, glancing back once as the door closed.

Sophie turned to Jessica. "It isn't like I'd sell something for a dollar instead of a hundred dollars." She shrugged.

"No. You seem to understand about the pricing. And it isn't as though you could find a mystery here in the next half hour."

Sophie grinned. "Actually, there is a mystery."

"Oh no!" Could Sophie find a new mystery in this short of a time?

Sophie motioned for Jessica to follow her to the back room. "Don't worry. I can't get into trouble with this. It's just that the floor seems hollow right here." She stomped her foot on the wood floor. "Mr. Braden, the owner of the boat store, used to play professional football and is a big guy. When he visits Mom, he won't step here because he says he's afraid he'll fall through."

Jessica walked over, stomped there, then stomped in a few other places. "You're right. It doesn't sound like the rest of the floor." She leaned against the shelves and watched as Sophie stomped again.

"Huh. It sounds stranger than usual. Kind of hollow. Maybe there's a secret passage under here."

"Sophie." Jessica rolled her eyes. "Next you'll tell me there's a secret passage to somewhere like Narnia. It's probably just an old floor that's getting worn-out."

Sophie jumped high up in the air, landing with both feet on the spot.

"No! What if it cracks?" Jessica cried out.

A crunching, creaking sound came from beneath Sophie's feet, and Jessica watched her cousin disappear through the floor.

"Aaaahhhhh!" Sophie screamed.

19

Underground Escape

"Sophie? You okay?" Jessica called out. "Sophie?"

"Just a second," said a faint voice Jessica barely recognized. She started to run toward the phone to call for an ambulance.

"I'm okay."

She stopped.

"That would have been much easier with stairs," the quiet voice said. "Please get the flashlight so I can see what's down here."

"Where is it?"

"Under the cash register," Sophie said more loudly, sounding more like herself already.

Jessica ran over to the counter, found a yellow plastic flashlight, and ran back. She pushed the button on the outside and stood a few feet from the hole, shining the light through it as well as she could from there.

"Can you bring it closer?" Sophie shouted.

Jessica lay down and scooted closer to the hole. "Does that help?"

Sophie shouted back, "Yes. I can see that I'm lying on a big fabric thing that's soft. But I still can't see what's around me. Can you point the light straight through the hole for a few seconds?"

"I'll try," Jessica shouted back. She edged a few inches closer and held her hand over the hole, pointing the light straight down.

"That's perfect."

Jessica felt one of the boards under her crack. Everything moved in slow motion as she slid through the hole. The floor of Great Finds moved by; then she was surrounded by darkness. *Whap!* She hit bottom.

"You okay?"

Jessica wheezed in air. Her chest hurt, but she could breathe. That had to be the scariest thing ever. Wiggling each leg and arm, Jessica declared, "Everything seems to work."

Sophie scooted next to her. "I found the flashlight." She clicked the button.

Jessica squeezed her eyes shut. "But there's a bright light in my eyes."

"Oh, sorry." Sophie moved the light to the side. "Fortunately, the flashlight landed on the other side of me, not on my head. At least we're both okay." She shined the light through the hole in the floor. "It's a long way up."

Jessica stared up at the hole filled with light from the shop. She could feel Sophie moving around like she was going to get up. "I think we should stay right here until someone comes to help us. We seem safe here."

"This *is* soft."

"But it's kind of smelly. You know, it's strange how nice this feels under us. Like a pile of mattresses. What's it look like in the light?"

Sophie shined the light all around the thing they'd landed on.

Jessica sat up. "If it didn't sound so strange, I'd say this was a pile of comforters." She pressed against it with her hand. "It's almost as fluffy as a stack of down comforters."

"Hey!" Sophie cried out.

Jessica jumped. "What? What?"

"Maybe this is filled with down. Someone from the Down Shoppe could have put it here."

Jessica put her hand on her racing heart. "You scared me. Don't *do* that. Besides, the Down Shoppe is almost a block away. How could they get it here? And who would be stupid enough to hide evidence under your mom's shop? I'll bet everyone knows you're working on the mystery."

"They might be smart criminals, not stupid. Until now, there was no door into the basement, so this was very safe. It might help solve the mystery."

Jessica groaned. "The smelly thing we were lucky enough to land on to prevent broken bones can't be a clue." She looked completely around them. Something looked back. "Sophie." She gestured behind them with her thumb.

"What's so important? I'm solving the mystery."

"A rat."

"Where?" Sophie asked nervously.

"There." Jessica pointed. Creepy just got creepier.

"If you're pointing, I can't see you." Sophie shined the light in Jessica's direction, then to where she pointed.

"There are *two* sets of eyes. Maybe we *should* try to get out of here."

"Mom said she'd be back in forty-five minutes. I fell through the floor right after she left, so we've probably got a half hour left before she'll be here to help us."

"Let's get up and walk around, shining the light on the walls as we go. Maybe there's another way out of here. A ladder or something."

"Deal."

Jessica watched her cousin rise, then slowly got up off the comforter herself. "I'm relieved that everything works while I'm standing, too."

Sophie lifted each arm and moved it around. "Me too. Let's go."

Standing in the middle of the room, they turned around slowly, the light revealing stone walls with a door on the left and the right sides.

Sophie actually seemed to hesitate. "Should we try one of them and see what's on the other side?"

"I'm surprised you'd stop to ask."

"You're right. We seem safe here, and who knows what's through that door. We should probably stay here." Sophie shined the light up to the ceiling and around the room one more time.

Jessica took a deep breath of the stale basement air, then regretted it. Coughing, she said, "There are rats here. Isn't the travel agency next to Great Finds on one side and the fur shop on the other?" *Calm, try to stay calm.*

"Oh, that's good. We know what's above it, so it should be safe just like here."

"Yep. I'll be brave." Jessica hurried to the door that led to the fur shop's basement and tried the doorknob. "It's locked."

Sophie followed her and tried it. "This won't budge. Let's try the other one."

With Sophie behind her, Jessica ran across the room, keeping an eye on the rat corner. Twisting that knob, she said, "It moved a little."

"Let me try." Sophie handed her the flashlight and grabbed the doorknob with both hands, twisting hard. After a few seconds, it gave way and the door opened with a spooky, creaking sound.

Jessica gulped. Then she nervously shined the light through the doorway. "It's like here. Empty." The light played off the wall on the other side of the room.

"Another door. You want to keep going or wait for my mom?"

Jessica glanced around. It seemed like almost anyplace would be better than where she was. "I'd like to get out of here."

"Me too." Sophie put her arm through Jessica's. "Let's go together."

Something skittered away into the corner of the Great Finds basement. "Yuck. Let's hurry." She returned the flashlight to Sophie. "If something small and furry bumps me, I might drop this and run."

The second door opened easily, and the girls soon found themselves in another empty basement, this time with a red door on the opposite side.

Sophie said, "There's a men's clothing store above here. Let's keep going."

Sophie stopped in front of the third door. "You know, I can't figure out where that door leads." Sophie shined the light on the door. "The men's clothing store is on a corner, so the street should be above whatever's through here."

"Do we go back or keep going?" Jessica didn't really want to do either. She just wanted to be back at ground level. "I hear the sound of tiny feet scurrying behind me." She rushed over, reached for the doorknob, and opened it.

Sophie shined the light inside.

"It's a tunnel," Jessica exclaimed. "The walls are made from blocks of stone and curved to make the tunnel round."

"I'd think this was really great almost any other time."

While Sophie shined the light around the walls, something bumped into Jessica's leg. "Let's get out of here." When Sophie stepped into the tunnel, Jessica followed close behind. "I don't know if we're breaking any laws, but you've got the light, so I'm with you."

At the end of the tunnel, shadows lined the walls. Sophie said, "I see some stuff piled in the corner, but I don't know which direction the tunnel took us in, so I'm not sure whose shop it would be near."

Jessica didn't care overly much about what it might be. She took a few more steps into the tunnel, but the light stayed back with Sophie. Her cousin shined the light into the corner, where Jessica could barely make out the shadows of some long, sticklike things.

Sophie said, "I would normally want to see what they were, but I just want to keep going and get out of here."

At the end of the tunnel, they faced yet another door. "There's only one way to find out what's in there." Jessica gulped, then turned the knob, while Sophie shined the light on it. "It's locked."

"No! It's got to open." Tucking the flashlight under her arm, Sophie pulled on the door. It creaked a little. "I think it's just old and rusty." She handed the flashlight to Jessica, then braced her feet on the ground and pulled. The door slowly creaked open and a feather blew out.

"Uh, Sophie," Jessica whispered as she looked up a well-lit stairway, "the Down Shoppe might be through this door."

"Uh-oh." Sophie peered through the doorway, then stepped back. "I think this is a way out, and all that light is sunlight coming through windows upstairs." The floor above them creaked. Sophie whispered, "Someone's up there."

Jessica whispered back, "Let's go up the stairs very quietly and see if we can sneak out. I'd rather be outside than in here."

"Me too. There's a wall next to the stairs, so I *think* we'll be safe."

"Who goes first?" Jessica felt her legs start to shake as she thought about who and what might be upstairs.

"I will."

Jessica watched Sophie gently step on each stair. Almost at the top, Sophie stopped and seemed to relax a bit, then waved Jessica on.

Just a few steps up, when Jessica could almost see out the windows, a woman spoke.

"George, I tell you, this isn't working."

Sophie backed against the wall. Jessica froze, with her right foot on one step and her left foot in midair.

20

Jessica's Secret

When Jessica opened her mouth to speak, Sophie shook her head and held her finger over her lips. Sophie was right. They probably would hear even a whisper this close.

"Eva, it *will* work. Give it time."

There were two people in the room, not just one on the phone talking to someone. The man's voice sounded so close that Jessica felt like she could reach out and touch him if the wall weren't between them.

When the woman spoke again, she sounded as if she'd moved closer. "We've run out of time. We'd be fine if you hadn't taken the down."

"They didn't know what they had," the man snarled.

The woman laughed shrilly. "But you made them wonder about it when you took it."

"I wouldn't have lost it in the first place if you hadn't told me to stay at that motel. When it was full, I took that terrible path through the forest in the middle of the night and tripped over a root."

"Then you almost finished it for us when you dumped the feathers in the window display."

"But Eva, that's *why* we wanted them in the first place."

"Not anymore. Those kids were making people suspicious."

A loud thump was followed by the words, "I'm getting some fresh air."

He'd see them if he looked back as he opened the door. Jessica slinked down the stairs. At the bottom, she carefully slipped through the door and took off running. Sophie was right behind her. Two minutes later they were back where they started, staring up at the hole Sophie'd made in the floor. The light from the flashlight suddenly dimmed and flickered.

"Oh, no. The batteries are low. What—"Jessica stopped talking when the bell from the shop door rang. She could hear footsteps on the floor above them.

"I hope it's Mom. We're here!" Sophie called.

"Where?" her mom called back.

"Go into the storeroom," Sophie yelled.

The footsteps stopped nearby. "Soph? Did you fall through that hole?"

The flashlight went dark. Jessica thumped it a couple of times, but it wouldn't come back on.

"Mom, help! Get us out of here."

"And hurry," Jessica whispered. "There's a rat convention going on here."

Sophie turned toward the rat area and saw four sets of eyes. "Yuck."

"Are you girls okay, or do you need a doctor?"

"We're fine, Mom. We landed on something soft."

Footsteps moved overhead. Then Jessica could hear bits and pieces of a conversation. The footsteps quickly came back toward them, and then Mrs. Sandoval peered through the hole at them.

Sophie shouted, "Be careful, Mom. Don't get too close."

Mrs. Sandoval stepped out of sight. "The sheriff is on her way."

"Good." Jessica sighed.

A few minutes later, she heard footsteps and voices, then a bright light shined through the hole, and someone lowered a rope with a loop in it to them.

Sheriff Valeska said, "One of you, slip the loop over your head and under your arms. Let me know when you're ready."

The rope landed on Jessica's lap, so she slipped it on. "Ready." The rope harness became taut, and her feet dangled off the ground as someone lifted her up. Back in the storeroom, she discovered both the sheriff and one of her deputies. "I am *so* happy to see you."

Jessica quickly crawled away from the hole, then stood and pulled off the rope. It vanished down the hole. Then they pulled Sophie up in it.

With the two of them sitting off to the side, Sheriff Valeska studied the area around the hole. "I can't figure out what happened to the floor. The rest of it appears quite solid."

Jessica pointed at the hole. "It seemed hollow where it broke."

Mrs. Sandoval said, "Sophie and I both knew there was something odd about the floor there. Bill Braden wouldn't stand in that spot because it seemed weak."

"Makes sense. What did you do, Sophie?" Sheriff Valeska asked suspiciously, turning toward her.

All eyes looked her way. "Why is everyone staring at me?" Sophie fidgeted nervously.

They continued to stare at her. Mrs. Sandoval tapped her foot on the floor.

Sophie, staring first at the floor, then at the ceiling, said, "Okay. So I wanted to know why the floor felt hollow."

Sheriff Valeska turned to Jessica. "So she jumped on it?"

"Weeellllll, . . ." Jessica hedged.

"You mean you did this on purpose?" Mrs. Sandoval reeled backward.

"Weeellllll, . . ." Sophie stared at the floor.

"Sophie Eileen, you are going to be punished. You won't know what's going on around town for a while because you'll be at home gardening and cooking and cleaning."

Sophie didn't argue. "Can you shine a light through the hole again?"

Mrs. Sandoval said, "Forget it, Sophie. It's time to go home."

"*Please?*"

Sheriff Valeska flipped on a floodlight she'd positioned over the hole. "It looks like a pile of down comforters." The sheriff sounded surprised.

Sophie turned to Jessica. "Trust me. We know they're soft."

"They can't be, but they look clean from here," Sheriff Valeska added. She turned toward her deputy, "Bruce, get Oscar McBride to unlock the door to his basement and go down his stairs to recover whatever they landed on."

"Through the fur shop?" Mrs. Sandoval asked. "Don't you mean through this hole?"

"No. Most of the basements are connected through the town. A hundred years ago, everyone knew that, but not many people know today." Sheriff Valeska gathered her rope and light. "Oscar McBride has stairs and locks his basement door. He says that he doesn't want just anyone going through his basement, and that makes sense since he has a lot of expensive fur coats in his store."

"Uh, Sheriff," Jessica called out just as the sheriff was pulling open the door, "we went through the basements and into the Down Shoppe."

The sheriff turned back toward them. "Trespassing, huh?"

"More like sitting in a dark basement with rats and really wanting to leave."

"I'll have Bruce check and make sure that all the doors are closed. I'm sure the other store owners will forgive you."

Jessica sighed. "Thanks, Sheriff."

The sheriff put her hand back on the door.

"But there is one more thing," Sophie said.

Sheriff Valeska paused. "What would that be, Sophie?"

"We heard the people in the Down Shoppe talking about stealing the briefcase from the police station."

"Think carefully. What were their exact words?"

Sophie repeated what they'd said.

"You heard the man say that he took the down and that he shouldn't have. We need something more concrete than that. While it might be criminal, it might not."

The sheriff left quickly, probably so no one could ask her any more questions.

"Okay, girls," Mrs. Sandoval said, "go home and take showers. What you landed on may have been soft but"—she sniffed at the air—"you stink."

Sophie laughed. "I'm so relieved that we're safe at street level that I'm going home without another word."

"And when you finish cleaning up . . ."

"Yes?" Sophie asked.

"Stay there."

Sophie sighed. "Will do. And," she added excitedly, "we can think about the evidence at home."

Jessica rolled her eyes. "She's unstoppable. Let's go to your house, Miss Stinky."

"Me? What about you?" Sophie sniffed the air as they went out the door.

Walking down the sidewalk, Jessica went through everything that had happened from the moment she fell through the hole to the rescue. "You know, Soph—"

"Hey, I think that's the first time you called me Soph."

"Oh, sorry. You know, Sophie—"

"I like being called Soph."

"Okay. I save a whole syllable." Jessica grinned.

"What were you going to say?"

"Oh yes. Those down comforters were soft, but not as soft as the one I have at home. It felt like they'd put harder feathers—"

"Yes!" Sophie exclaimed. "Not like the feathers we found in the briefcase."

"Exactly. If I was going to make a down comforter, and I'd never been around feathers—only seen a picture of them—I might think any feathers would work."

"You're right. They might have made the comforters with the wrong feathers, and when they didn't turn out soft and fluffy, they had to get rid of them." Sophie snapped her fingers. "That cinches it. The Down Shoppe is a phony."

"*If* they made the comforters. I wonder why the people from the Down Shoppe would drag them all the way over here. Maybe they're from the business that was in this location before your mom owned it. Maybe they sold comforters and just stored them there."

"It was a bookstore. And remember that they were clean, not rat-messed up, so they're newer. I just know the comforters are a clue." Sophie paced across the room. "We have to get Mom to let us out of the house tomorrow so we can see what Deputy Bruce pulled out of the basement."

Jessica wrinkled her nose. "I hope he puts some of the feathers in a plastic bag. That thing we were lying on smelled terrible."

After dinner, Jessica started in the direction of their room. "Tonight's a good night to read. It's quiet and calm. How's that sound to you?"

"I'm reading a great spy thriller," Sophie said as she followed her.

Jessica shuddered as they entered the bedroom. "How can you read that stuff when real bad guys are chasing us?"

"The book isn't real, and I know that. That man who chased us the other day was real. This takes my mind off him."

"It makes sense in a strange way."

Sophie threw her pillow at Jessica.

"Hey, you'll mess my hair." Jessica patted her hair with her hands, then threw the pillow back at her.

Sophie giggled. "I'm so glad you don't care about your hair and makeup as much as you did when you got here."

"Me too. I can even be smart here."

Jessica clamped her hand over her mouth.

"What?" Sophie giggled. "You aren't any smarter than I am." Then she paused and stared at Jessica. "But you do use very large words sometimes."

"Forget I said anything." Jessica sat down on her bed and pretended to read. Maybe Sophie would just pick up her book.

Sophie sat on the edge of her bed. "Are you really a brainy type?"

No chance Sophie would ignore what she'd said. Jessica cringed as she answered, "Yes."

"I should have suspected as much. Sometimes you seemed smart. I remember when you first read the papers. You seemed to know what you were reading. Did you?"

Jessica looked down. "A lot of it."

"Why do you hide being smart?"

As tears filled her eyes, Jessica tried to blink them away. "Please, please don't tell anyone, Sophie. People think that you're supposed to wear ugly clothes and sit alone in the corner when you're smart. No one will like me anymore."

"Dry those eyes, Cousin. No one here will treat you any differently." Sophie went back to her bed and threw her pillow again, ducking when Jessica threw it right back at her. "Although I may call you during the school year and have you help me with my homework."

Jessica smiled. "As you would say, 'Deal.' I felt like I was living a lie. At least I can be myself here." Jessica got into her pajamas, under the covers, and happily started reading for real this time.

21

The Wrong Feathers

Sophie pushed aside the curtain on the front window of the house, letting in the light of a bright, sunny day. This would be a great day to be hiking, but with Jessica she would have suggested the beach. They were trapped in the house instead.

"Mom, can we—"

"No, Sophie."

"But, Mom, we can't stay here all day every day."

Her mother stopped polishing a silver teapot. Glancing up at the big grandfather clock in the corner, she said. "The carpenter should be finished with the floor by now, so we can go to Great Finds."

"We get to leave the house?"

"Jessica's not being punished, so I could let her leave anytime, but I want the two of you together at all times."

"Yippee!" Sophie hollered.

"Hang on. You have to stay with me in Great Finds. Or your father or I, or another adult we've approved, has to be with you." She held up her hand when Sophie started to speak. "Don't bother to argue. With criminals running around, your father and I agreed this was what we needed to do. Besides, you're grounded right now."

Sophie and Jessica went into the bedroom, and Jessica changed into what she called "more suitable clothes" to wear to Great Finds. Sophie stayed as she was—jeans and a T-shirt. As they were leaving, Sophie grabbed the papers out of her box.

Jessica rolled her eyes. "What do you want with those? We've looked and looked at them. The FBI doesn't even care about them because Agent Dallas didn't pick them up."

"Maybe we can find time to look again. I figure if we solve this crime, then the FBI and the sheriff will take away the bad guys. I love a mystery, but being watched and staying inside all the time is too much."

"This is one time when I like the way your mind works." Jessica grinned. "Aunt April's shop is okay, but . . ."

Mrs. Sandoval called from the kitchen, "Girls, since you're going to be at Great Finds every day, I'm going to pay you."

"Excellent!" Sophie exclaimed.

"Being there just got better."

They met Mrs. Sandoval in the living room. "Don't get too excited. It won't be a lot, but it will buy you some new things for school this fall."

As they drove to the antique shop, Jessica excitedly said, "New clothes, Sophie."

Clothes would be fairly low on Sophie's list of priorities. "What I have is fine."

Jessica put out her foot. "Maybe shoes?"

Sophie shrugged. "Nothing for school—but new hiking boots would be good."

"We're definitely different."

Sophie grinned. "You got that right, Cousin."

The carpenter was packing up his tools when they arrived.

"Thanks for the quick work, Joe."

"Happy to be of service, April. The place your daughter crashed through was a basement access that had been covered up years ago. I repaired the damage and added a hinged door." He put his hammer in the toolbox.

"Funny thing is . . ." His voice trailed off as he spoke and stared at the floor, shaking his head. Then he focused on Mrs. Sandoval again. "The underside of the floor looked altered in an odd way. It sounds impossible, but it seemed that somebody cut it. And recently. That's why Sophie was able to crash through so easily."

"So it wasn't completely my fault?" A glimmer of hope that her grounding would be lifted flickered into Sophie's mind.

"Don't think you can get off easily, Sophie. You still jumped on it, and that's why it broke."

Glimmer extinguished.

Mrs. Sandoval checked out the new door. "Joe, I don't see how it's possible that someone cut the floor. Maybe it just appeared to have been cut."

He said, "Maybe." But Sophie didn't think he was buying that idea.

"I made a ladder so you could go down there. Will that do? I could come back and make you some stairs."

Mrs. Sandoval peered down the hole into the basement. "Let's try the ladder and see how it works. I need to get Hank the electrician to install a light in there."

"There already is one, from the days when the basement was used."

"A light?" Jessica asked. "We sat in the dark, and a light was waiting to be turned on?"

"You couldn't have reached it, but I made the chain longer so you could now. When you're on the ladder, reach to the right and feel for the pull chain." Joe climbed into the hole. "Oh, and I had the exterminator come, and the rats are all gone. It'll just take me a few minutes in the basement to finish up."

Sophie suddenly had a not-so-happy vision of trips up and down the ladder with merchandise in her arms. Her mom had talked about more storage space for years.

Just then, Mrs. Bowman came into the shop, carrying a yellow box.

Mrs. Sandoval said, "I didn't want you to think I'd completely forgotten about you, girls. I called Bananas and asked Abigail Bowman if she would do us a favor and bring over some of her banana-blueberry muffins for a snack."

Mrs. Bowman set down the box and left. Then the girls each grabbed a muffin.

Sophie said, "Wow. Thanks, Mom."

"Yes, thank you, Aunt April."

After eating, Mrs. Sandoval gave them chores to do.

Almost three hours later, Sophie came over to where Jessica was working on a project. "How's it going?"

Jessica blew her hair off her face and groaned. "This will take forever."

Sophie nodded. "Mom must believe that as long as she's paying us, we can get some bigger projects done for her."

"*We?* This one's all *me* right now. Hurry."

"I'll clean as fast as I can." As she went out front, Sophie said, "Mom, it must be time for lunch."

Mrs. Sandoval checked her watch. "It is. It's one o'clock. You and Jessica only have permission to go to the deli. I can clearly see you walking over there. Get your lunch and bring it back here. But call me before you return so I can watch you."

"The deli's fine." Jessica's grin almost split her face.

A few minutes later, Tony put their lunches in a paper bag. "I hear you made an entrance to the basement under Great Finds."

"Very funny." Sophie unwrapped her straw, put it in her soda, and took a sip.

"How'd you know?" Jessica asked.

Tony looked over at Sophie and smiled.

Jessica answered her own question. "It's that small-town thing again, right? The whole town knows?"

"Probably. Were there a lot of rats?" Tony asked.

Jessica shuddered. "Yes. I was so glad to get out of there."

"And Sophie, I hear your mom won't let you out of her sight." Tony continued grinning.

"But that's because . . ." Jessica started, then stopped and looked at Sophie.

Sophie jumped in. "You're right, Tony. I've spent a lot of time dusting. Need anything dusted? I've become an expert."

Tony laughed. "No thanks. I'm the youngest, so I'm the duster here."

"Can I use your phone? Mom wants me to call when we're coming back."

"Whew. She sure is watching you. Here." Tony handed Sophie the phone, then turned to Jessica. "Maybe you'll get to eat here next time and I can make those sundaes."

Jessica got a silly grin.

As they left the deli, Sophie said, "You almost told. Again."

Jessica frowned. "I'm sorry, but I stopped before I said anything too suspicious."

Back at Great Finds, a plan formed in Sophie's mind as they ate. Their next step would be to see the feathers from the comforters they'd landed on.

"Mom, you must want to visit your friend the sheriff," she said, once they'd resumed working.

"Not right now." Her mom rearranged some yellow flowers in a blue glass vase. Then she placed some teacups with painted flowers on them next to the vase.

Sophie paced the shop. "Maybe Dad has something he needs at the sheriff's office."

"I doubt it."

"Can I—"

Her mother raised her hands. "I give up. The sheriff's office isn't far. You're in the public eye in town. Go. Quickly."

Sophie called, "Jessica, let's go."

Jessica came out of the back room, pushing her hair out of her face. "Huh?"

"Mom's letting us go to the sheriff's office."

"Great." Jessica ran to the bathroom, and came back with her hair neatly combed.

Sheriff Valeska picked a clear plastic bag full of feathers up off her desk when Sophie and Jessica walked through the door. "I can guess why you girls are here." Handing it to Sophie, she said, "Once again, you've found the evidence, so I'll let you see it."

Sophie turned the bag from side to side, studying this clue. When she handled evidence, she felt like a real detective. She handed it to her cousin.

Without reaching into the bag, Jessica shifted the feathers around to separate one from another. "When I press against these feathers, they're harder and they aren't anywhere near as fluffy as those in the briefcase."

Sheriff Valeska leaned back in her chair and said, "That's an excellent observation. Since the expert at Fish and Game was on vacation, I sent over a scan of a few of them to a professor of ornithology at the college, and he said they were chicken feathers."

Sophie turned them into the light. "They aren't the right feathers for a down comforter. Only someone who was a phony would make a down comforter out of hard chicken feathers. Every clue points more and more to the Down Shoppe as a criminal hangout." Sophie stared at the floor while she paced back and forth across the room. "The question is, why would someone do this? What does it all mean?"

Jessica stepped in front of her and put one hand on each shoulder. Sophie looked her in the eyes and Jessica said,

"You're making assumptions again based on something that might be a coincidence."

"What? Please speak English."

"You're guessing. Oh, and you asked two questions again."

Sophie grinned. "This is a solid clue. Right, Sheriff?"

The sheriff said, "Those comforters aren't there for any logical reason we know of, so I think they are. You didn't find them in the usual way, but I guess I should thank you anyway."

They came back the long way, around the block, instead of taking the more direct, shorter route to Great Finds. Sophie wasn't breaking rules—because they didn't stop— but it gave her a little more time outside.

As they passed Simpson's Shoes, Mr. Simpson was standing in front and said, "I understand you're solving mysteries for the sheriff."

Sophie laughed.

"We have a mystery here at Simpson's Shoes."

22

Unlocking A Mystery

Jessica's heart dropped to the ground. "*Another* mystery in Pine Hill?"

"Yes, and we're puzzled by it. Why would anyone keep unlocking our doors at night?"

Sophie jumped right on it. "Sounds interesting. Let's ask Mom if we can come over and help."

The two of them ran over to Great Finds where Sophie's mom quickly agreed that Simpson's Shoes would be a safe place.

They hurried back, then followed Mr. Simpson into his shoe store. He asked, "What do you think of the new window display, girls?"

"Very pretty. I like these shoes." Jessica touched her finger to a pair of navy flats.

"Nice choice."

He seemed ready to say more about what Jessica thought was a display filled with beautiful shoes, but Sophie couldn't stand the delay. "Show us what's happened," she said with excitement.

Mr. Simpson said, "I'll give you the chance to solve this mystery. Twice now, we've come in and found the front door and the door to the storeroom unlocked. We had the locks changed the first time, but whoever it was opened them again."

"Is anything missing?"

"Barely anything. A doorstop and one pair of women's shoes. That's another strange part of this."

Jessica asked, "What kind of shoes?"

"High heels. Red leather. Size 8."

"Let's look around, Jessica." Sophie turned toward Mr. Simpson. "If you don't mind."

"Please do. I know the sheriff didn't find any clues, but since you've been helping her, maybe you can find a clue here."

Jessica whispered as they walked away, "He thinks we're a combination of Nancy Drew and the head of the FBI."

Sophie laughed.

Jessica checked out the shoes as she walked through.

"See anything?"

"A lot of shoes I want."

Sophie groaned. "This isn't a shopping trip. We're detectives."

Jessica giggled. "There's always time to shop. There are so many shoes. It's like heaven for a shoe lover."

"Mystery. Think mystery."

"Okay. Okay." After checking under and around everything, Jessica said, "Not a shoelace out of place."

"Very neat. If there had been a clue, the Simpsons probably swept it away by now."

"I wonder what's through there." Jessica pointed at a door in the back of the room.

"Let's find out." Sophie walked over and put her hand on the doorknob.

"Shouldn't we ask Mr. Simpson if it's okay to open it?"

"He said we should look around. This is part of *around*." Sophie opened the door and flipped on a light switch just inside. "Stairs. Maybe they have a basement."

Both girls stared down the stairs for a minute, then at each other.

"Do you think?" Jessica said.

Rushing downstairs, Sophie said, "Maybe there's a door into the tunnels."

"My thought exactly." Jessica followed her.

At the bottom they found a large door.

"Let's see what's in here." Sophie turned the doorknob.

Jessica put out her hand to stop her. "There might be rats waiting to run in here."

"No," Sophie said. "They'll stay where it's dark."

"Yuck." Jessica cringed and cautiously watched the door open. No rats.

"Hey!" Sophie reached through the doorway for something on the floor. "It's a doorstop, probably the missing doorstop. But why would someone take a doorstop from upstairs and use it down here?"

Jessica closed then reopened the door. "It's like the door leading into our garage at home. It closes by itself if you let go."

"Ah, so they had to prop it open to move something in or out of here."

"Exactly."

"But what were they moving?"

"Did you girls find something?" Mr. Simpson asked from the top of the stairs.

"Your doorstop. Do you have a flashlight?"

"I'll get it for you." He hurried away.

Sophie pushed the doorstop under the door. "Why would they use this to come through here when they can easily come and go through their own building? They only took one pair of shoes, so they must not have come here to steal."

"They must have been hiding from someone."

"Could be. Or maybe they just didn't want to be seen near their building but didn't mind being seen outside another one."

"Very good. Could be either." An image of rats' eyes glowing in the dark popped into Jessica's mind. "I hope Mr. Simpson has a large flashlight. I don't want to be the guest of honor at another gathering of rodents."

"You have got a point there." Sophie stood proudly. "I told you Simpson's Shoes was a clue."

"I agree with you. Now."

Mr. Simpson returned with two large flashlights and handed one to each of them. "What are you going to use them for?"

"We're going to check out what's beyond here." Sophie pointed at the now propped-open door.

He shrugged. "It's a basement we rarely use."

"We'd still like to see what's there."

"Must we?" Jessica asked.

Sophie looked at her and Jessica sighed. She knew the answer. "We must."

"Shouldn't we call the sheriff?" Mr. Simpson asked.

"We've been in the basements before," Sophie said as she stepped inside. They found a door on one side of the room, opened it, and shining the light inside, found a rounded tunnel like the one they'd been in before.

"Do you think it's the same one?" Jessica asked.

"Think about it. We aren't under the men's shop, so it can't be."

"Good point. Maybe there are lots of them connecting everything under the streets."

Cars drove by overhead as the girls moved through the tunnel. At the end of the tunnel, another door led them into a basement.

"I remember this red door," Jessica said as they walked into the room. "I think that now we're in the basement of the men's shop." She scraped golden dust off the floor with the toe of her shoe. "We have twice the light this time. Sophie, I think this is sawdust."

Sophie crouched and held her light over the dust. "You're right." Standing, she looked around the room.

"This store only has a hole for access, just like Great Finds, and the sawdust is right under it. I wonder if the owner closed off their basement access too."

Sophie nodded. "This means the carpenter had the right answer about why I fell through the floor. Someone tampered with the access here, so they probably did that under Mom's shop too."

"Exactly."

"Let's keep moving." Sophie pointed across the room. "That red door leads to another tunnel."

"What you mean is that it leads toward the Down Shoppe."

At the end of the tunnel, a familiar door was in front of them. Sophie put her hand on the doorknob. "I wonder if we could sneak inside and take a quick look around."

"Sophie! The sheriff would say that's breaking and entering."

"We'd be walking through a door that's probably still unlocked, so not breaking, just entering."

"I don't believe that makes it legal."

Behind them a door opened and closed. Then footsteps echoed through the tunnel, coming closer and closer by the second.

23

Inside, At Last

Jessica's heart pounded as she and Sophie crawled behind some of the stuff piled in the tunnel and turned off their flashlights. She shivered as the footsteps grew louder and louder, then stopped right in front of them.

"Sophie. Jessica."

Jessica let out a huge sigh of relief.

"We're here, Sheriff." Sophie stepped into the bright light of the sheriff's flashlight, and Jessica followed behind her.

"What are you two up to? Sophie?"

"We're on the trail of a clue."

"What clue? Mr. Simpson told me you found his doorstop."

"Yes. No. I mean, the doorstop was outside their basement door. Someone must have used it to prop it open. We wanted to see if the tunnel in his basement connected to the one that leads to the Down Shoppe." Sophie pointed at the door. "It does."

The sheriff sighed. "Even if the Down Shoppe people were guilty of something, you couldn't accuse them without evidence. And you shouldn't be here."

"Why not? You can hear cars driving overhead, so we're under the street. We're not on private property."

"Let's go, girls."

Sophie said, "What about all this fishing gear that's just laying here?"

"Huh?" the sheriff and Jessica asked.

"Remember the tall, skinny things in the shadows, Jessica?"

"Yes. But—"

"Those were fishing poles. I saw them when I ducked in here. There are also tackle boxes and a lot of other fishing things, like what we used on Captain Jack's boat."

All three shined their flashlights into the area.

Jessica stepped closer. "When we were here before, there were more of the tall, skinny things that I now know are fishing poles. I think they've gotten rid of a bunch of them."

"Yes, ladies. This is strange, but it doesn't prove guilt. It just makes me wonder why all this valuable property is here. It could be sold for a tidy sum of money." The sheriff shined her flashlight back the way they'd come. "Time to go."

"Look here," Jessica called. She ran over and picked up something from the floor.

"It's just an empty shoe box," the sheriff said.

"Not just any empty shoe box. Mr. Simpson said that whoever unlocked their doors stole a pair of red, size 8 high heels." She shined her flashlight on the end of the box. "There's a picture of red high heels, and it says size 8."

The sheriff took the box and tucked it under her arm. "This *is* an important clue. I'd assumed the Down Shoppe owners had rented their space from the building's owners. That happens all the time in business, but none of this makes sense." She looked at the door to the Down Shoppe. "I would love to go inside, but I'd lose my job. Let's go back, girls. I hope we find something soon that is big enough to talk a judge into issuing a search warrant."

Sophie and Jessica followed the sheriff back to Simpson's Shoes. When they arrived, Mr. Simpson was waiting in the basement.

"Did you discover something?" he asked.

Sophie looked up at the sheriff.

"We have suspicions, but nothing confirmed," the sheriff said.

"I think you'll know more soon, Mr. Simpson," Sophie added.

Back at the antique shop, while Jessica dusted and Sophie cleaned, Sophie told her mother what they'd seen. Before long, it was time to go home. When they were heading out the door, Sophie grabbed the box of leftover muffins.

As Mrs. Sandoval locked the door, she said, "I'm surprised Sam and Charlotte sold the business."

"Huh?" Sophie turned toward her mother.

"The building the Down Shoppe is in was a fishing shop last year. Remember, Sophie? Hook, Line & Sinker?"

"That's right. I only went there once, when we bought Dad a new fishing pole for his birthday."

Mrs. Sandoval chewed on her lip. "The business owners, Sam and Charlotte Cross, actually owned the building their shop was in. They weren't just renting it. When they closed for the winter, they told me that they would reopen in the spring for the fishing season. You could see all of their fishing gear through the window so I assumed they'd come back when they could."

"Do *you* know where they're living? The sheriff didn't mention that she did. Otherwise I think she would have called them," Jessica said.

Mrs. Sandoval stabbed at the air with her finger. "Yes, I do." She turned back into the store, walked over to the phone, flipped through a small notebook sitting next to it, then dialed. "Charlotte?" she said, seconds later. "This is April Sandoval in Pine Hill . . . Yes, thank you. We were surprised you'd sold or rented your store and wanted to check on you . . . What? . . . Someone *is* in there, with a sign out front saying, 'The Down Shoppe.'" She gave the phone number for the sheriff, then said good-bye.

Turning back to the girls, she said, "It's supposed to be their shop and closed until they can return. They had to attend to a family emergency and weren't able to come back in the spring."

"Wow! So Sheriff Valeska can go in." Sophie jumped up and down. "Yes, yes, yes!"

"But Sam and Charlotte want to drive here first so they can see what's going on."

Jessica could feel the mystery ramping up. "Sophie, if we can figure out why the doors on Simpson's Shoes are being unlocked, we'll have this solved." Solve the mystery, have a simple summer vacation. Not that anything about her stay in Pine Hill had been simple, but she could hope.

Sophie leaned against the counter. "I think I know about the doors."

"Are you sure?" Jessica asked.

Mrs. Sandoval paused. "Okay, what's the reason?"

"The phony Down Shoppe people needed to get rid of the fishing shop products, and they didn't want to take them out through their door. People might think it was strange that all the fishing stuff was still there if Hook, Line & Sinker didn't plan to reopen."

Jessica got excited now. "So they're going through the basements and out Simpson's Shoes in the middle of the night."

"Yes."

"That does sound plausible, Soph," Mrs. Sandoval agreed. "But why do they need a phony Down Shoppe? Anyway, the Crosses said they'd be here tomorrow. I'll call Mandy Valeska and let her know." She picked up the phone again.

While her mom was busy, Sophie spoke softly to Jessica, "We should call Agent Dallas."

"We did the other day, and he hasn't called us back."

"True. Something must have happened to him. We have to rescue him."

"Seriously? *If* something has happened, the FBI must know that. You think that the entire FBI hasn't been able to help him, but we can?"

"Yep."

Jessica rolled her eyes. "What do you propose?"

"I'm working on it."

Mrs. Sandoval hung up the phone and said, "By the way, Jessica, Frank Avinson told me you were going to write an article for the *Pine Hill Press*. Remember all of the details about this. It will make an exciting story."

Jessica happily sank into a comfortable, old chair. "That's a superb suggestion. In fact, it's magnificent."

"Superb? Magnificent?" Sophie laughed.

"What happened to the way you usually speak?" Mrs. Sandoval asked.

"Our little Jessica has been hiding something from us. She's very, very smart."

"I've suspected that for a while." Mrs. Sandoval reached down and hugged Jessica. "I'm glad you trust us enough to be yourself."

Jessica felt even more relieved than when Sophie had found out. "Thank you, Aunt April. I felt like I was lying and didn't want to do it anymore."

Her aunt smiled. "Now you can help Sophie with her homework."

Sophie laughed. "I already told her that."

"You girls get your things and we'll go home."

As they rode home, both girls in the backseat, Sophie said, "The owners are coming here tomorrow, so we'll get new clues from inside the building and we might even solve the whole mystery."

Jessica answered, "I can't wait. When the mystery is solved, we can go to the beach, shop, and eat for the rest of the summer."

"And go for hikes," Sophie added.

"I'll have to think about that."

Just before 5 a.m., Sophie's parents got ready to meet the Crosses. The sheriff told them she, four FBI agents, and two deputies would also meet them at the Down Shoppe.

Unfortunately, when they were finishing breakfast, Mr. Sandoval said, "Stay here."

"Dad! How can you say that? We're the ones who found out about the Down Shoppe. We need to be there."

"Stay here." He grabbed his coat off the hook and put it on.

"Mom?" Sophie watched her mother put her coat on.

Mrs. Sandoval shook her head, and they left.

Sophie slumped down on the sofa. "This is so frustrating. Here we solve everything, then they leave us at home." She stood and circled the room. This was not how she'd pictured the end of the mystery. "Let's go upstairs. Maybe flashing lights from the sheriff's vehicles in town will show through the trees and we'll know that they're at the Down Shoppe."

The two girls stood at the windows that faced town.

Sophie couldn't see anything beyond the trees. "Nothing."

"No."

"Did you hear that?" Sophie asked.

Jessica stared at her. "What? Can you hear sirens?"

Sophie held her finger in front of her mouth. "Shh."

Downstairs, a creaking sound was followed by a thud.

24

Talking to Tony

Sophie motioned for Jessica to follow her across the hall, through another bedroom, and to a window.

Jessica whispered, "Do you think your parents are back already?"

"Uh-uh." Sophie pointed down the driveway to a black car partly hidden by trees. "I think all the sounds are coming from the front of the house. Let's sneak down the back stairs to the kitchen and go outside."

Her cousin went pale. "But Sophie, if they come into the kitchen, they'll see us."

Sophie nodded. "That's better than staying upstairs and not being able to get out if they come here. Be ready to run. As we walk, put your foot where I just put mine. I know where the floors creak in this old house."

Sophie could feel Jessica right behind her as she went down the hall, then crept down the stairs. Slowly, ever so slowly, she opened the door to the kitchen. Empty. Running across the room, they both reached for the doorknob on the back door, but Sophie got her hands on it first and jerked the door open. Out the door, she ran for the closest trees, with Jessica so close on her heels that she thought she might trip her. Sophie kept running until they'd circled the house. Then they crouched behind a large tree.

Jessica spoke in a low voice. "Maybe we can identify whoever comes out the door."

"My thoughts exactly."

A while later, Sophie guessed about ten minutes, the "French" woman from the Down Shoppe stepped out the front door of the house. And she was eating what looked like a leftover banana-blueberry muffin. "Maybe we should try to stop her."

The woman looked around, threw the muffin to the side, and ran to her car. Before they had a chance to do anything, she was backing out onto the road.

"Oops. I think she heard me."

"I think she did. I wonder why she came here." Jessica stood.

"Breakfast?"

Jessica giggled nervously.

When they stepped through the front door, they found a mess. Drawers and shelves were empty, with everything from them littering the floor.

Jessica picked up a sofa cushion and put it back where it belonged. "Amazing. She even pulled the cushions off the sofa."

"Criminals always do. At least she didn't slit them."

"Should we clean the room before your mom and dad come home?"

"I don't want to disturb the crime scene. But this is a mess, and Mom really hates messes. Normally I'd leave it for the sheriff, but this woman must have left plenty of fingerprints on everything else in the house, including the plastic bag Mom put the muffins in." Sophie reached for a pile of papers.

"Hey, let's take photos."

Sophie rolled her eyes. "Why didn't I think of that?" She ran to her room and came back with her camera.

Walking around the torn-apart sections of the house, she snapped dozens of photos. Done with that, Sophie said, "Now, we clean."

When her parents walked in the front door later, the house was almost back to normal.

"What's going on?" Mrs. Sandoval asked as soon as she saw Sophie with the vacuum.

"A woman broke in and took the place apart."

Mr. Sandoval stepped forward. "I'm going to make sure there's no one else here." He checked every room downstairs, then went upstairs.

"We saw her drive off, Dad." Sophie put the vacuum in the hall closet.

Mrs. Sandoval hugged Sophie, pulling Jessica into the hug. "Are you girls okay?"

Jessica said, "Yes. We ran out the kitchen door."

"I'm glad you're safe. Is anything missing?" Mrs. Sandoval looked around the room.

Sophie shrugged. "I don't think so. She wasn't carrying anything when she left."

"Except a muffin." Jessica giggled.

Mrs. Sandoval cringed. "She got into them after she got dirty searching the house? I'll be sure to get rid of the rest."

"We thought the police could use the plastic bag for her fingerprints."

Mrs. Sandoval nodded agreement. "We'll be careful not to touch it. Now let's call the sheriff."

Sophie suddenly remembered where her parents had gone. "Hey, what did the sheriff and FBI find in the Down Shoppe?"

"Other than more fingerprints, not much," Mrs. Sandoval answered.

Jessica jumped in. "I'm sure they'll match these. We think this is the same woman we saw in the Down Shoppe and around town."

Mrs. Sandoval sat down on the sofa. "The Down Shoppe was totally empty. Except for a few feathers. Sheriff Valeska said they were the same kind of large feathers that were in the comforters you landed on. It tied the comforters in with the people in there."

Sophie and Jessica sat next to her as Mr. Sandoval came down the stairs, shaking his head. "The upstairs rooms are fine. It's just the downstairs that she messed up."

Sophie already knew that, but her dad seemed to need to check it out himself. She asked, "What did Agent Dallas have to say when you saw him?"

"He didn't come."

"Did other FBI agents come?"

"His partner, Agent Able, and two other agents."

"Hmm. I wonder. . ." Sophie tapped her fingers on the arm of the sofa.

"You wonder what?" Jessica asked.

"I wonder where Agent Dallas is."

"Probably wherever the criminals are. Doing his job," Mrs. Sandoval answered.

"It seems strange that he wasn't there." Sophie couldn't understand why they'd take the agent off the case who knew the most about it.

Mrs. Sandoval stood. "Unless we decide to leave a sign at Great Finds that says, Out Catching Criminals, I think we'd better go to work."

Sophie laughed. "I like the sign idea."

"Can we get sandwiches from the deli today?" Jessica asked as they stood.

Mr. Sandoval asked, "Aren't you girls getting tired of sandwiches from the deli?"

"I am," Sophie said. "Last time, I had soup."

Mrs. Sandoval laughed. "They also have salads, Soph."

"Sandwiches are fine with me." Jessica grinned all the way to the deli when they were told they could go later.

They'd almost finished their lunches when Tony came over and asked what kind of sundaes they'd like. When he brought Jessica's hot fudge sundae and Sophie's pineapple sundae, he said, "You're our only customers right now, so I can talk for a minute. How's summer going?"

Jessica took a bite of her sundae, "Great! We're hot on the trail of some criminals."

Sophie dropped her spoon. "Jessica!"

"She's kidding, right?" Tony asked Sophie.

Jessica stuck her spoon in her sundae and swirled it through the hot fudge.

Sophie sighed. "What now, O wise one?"

Tony sat down, his eyes sparkling. "This sounds a lot more exciting than life in a deli. Tell me what's going on."

Jessica took a bite of her sundae, then looked at Tony. "We aren't supposed to tell about the FBI part—"

"Jessica! Eat and stop talking."

"The FBI? Here in Pine Hill?" Tony leaned forward in his chair.

Sophie took another bite of her sundae. What could they do now? "He knows enough that maybe we should tell him what's going on. Another point of view might be good."

Jessica nodded excitedly. "I've wanted to tell someone for the longest time. You're trustworthy, aren't you, Tony?"

"If you mean, will I tell this to anyone else? Nope."

"Okay. It all started with a briefcase we found on Cutoff Trail." Sophie told the story, with Jessica putting in pieces now and then.

When they'd finished, Tony sat back in his chair. "Wow! Your summer hasn't been dull."

"I think it only seemed really dangerous when a man sat down at our table in the resort. But he turned out to be an FBI agent."

"You skipped that part." Tony leaned forward again.

"Oh," Jessica went on, "he just wanted to know what we knew, but we didn't find out he was an FBI agent until later. We ran and hid in the tunnel behind the waterfall."

"Do you girls need help with your crime?"

Sophie and Jessica looked at each other. Jessica pleaded with her eyes for Tony to help them.

"Why don't you come over tonight," Sophie said.

Tony rubbed his hands together. "See you about seven."

Back at Great Finds, Jessica hummed as she cleaned.

"What's going on with your happy cousin?" her mother asked Sophie.

"Tony's coming over tonight to hear all about the bad guys."

Her mother placed the antique quilt she was holding on a shelf and turned around. "Sophie, you know you weren't supposed to tell."

"I know, but Jessica spilled it, and then it was too late."

"Do you think Tony can keep the secret?"

Sophie nodded. "I think so."

25

Operation Dallas

After the girls had gone through all their clues that night and told him about calling Agent Dallas, Tony asked, "Have you heard from him?"

"No. And we haven't seen him either."

"Strange," he muttered. Shrugging, he said, "It could be good news."

Jessica wondered if inviting Tony to help had been a big mistake. What he'd just said hadn't made any sense at all.

"Maybe he's so busy he doesn't have time to call," he added.

Now he made sense. "But for your idea to work, we have to assume he's been sent somewhere else. I'd think either they'd tell us that when we called or he'd call to explain."

"Or maybe he can't call," Sophie said.

"What?" Tony turned to Sophie.

"In the movies the bad guy takes the good guy hostage."

Tony laughed. "Too many movies." He twirled his finger next to his ear.

"Her idea may not be as crazy as it sounds," Jessica said. "I didn't think these things really happened when I arrived here. But after helping the FBI, I'm starting to think anything's possible."

Tony sighed. "I see your point. Let's call Agent Dallas again and see if he answers."

"It isn't as exciting as a rescue, but it does sound like the right thing to do," Sophie agreed.

A few minutes later Jessica hung up the phone. "This time they said he's late calling in for his messages. They took another message from me. If he isn't checking his messages . . ."

Sophie chewed on her lip. "Where would bad guys put an FBI agent?"

"Where would bad guys put themselves?" Jessica raised her hands and shrugged. "We haven't figured that much out."

"Is there a basement under the Down Shoppe?" Tony asked.

Sophie said, "When we walked through all the basements from Mom's antique shop to the Down Shoppe on our attempted escape, we opened a door that led to stairs going to the front door of the Down Shoppe. We weren't in a basement under the store, more like beside the building." She paused. "I don't think there could be a basement."

Tony got a cute, intense look. "If there are basements under your mom's side of the street and under our deli, too—"

"And under Simpson's Shoes," Jessica added.

"All the buildings were built about the same time—"

"So there should be one under the Down Shoppe, and maybe someone is hiding an FBI agent in it," Jessica said excitedly. "Good thinking, Tony!"

"We need to call Sheriff Valeska to learn more about this morning's search."

Sophie dialed and talked to her.

"So the FBI went over the building with a fine-tooth comb and didn't find a basement? . . . Thank you." Sophie sighed and hung up. She stood and walked across the room, then turned, walked back, and sat back down. A few seconds later, she got up and walked across the room again.

"Knock it off," Jessica said.

Sophie perched on the arm of the sofa. "I think we should go look anyway."

Jessica shrugged. "But Sheriff Valeska said—"

"I know what she said, but it would be really weird if every building we know of had a basement except that one."

"You're right, but how do we get in?" Tony asked.

"The owners went home but left the key with Mom and Dad, so it's easy to get inside."

"That's right," Jessica exclaimed.

Sophie said, "Now the only problem will be getting permission for 'Operation Dallas.'"

"Great name. It sounds official," Jessica agreed.

"I'll bet your parents will want the FBI to rescue their own man," Tony said.

"We called the FBI and got nowhere. We called the sheriff, and she says the law enforcement people searched and there is no basement. We have to do this ourselves."

Tony touched Jessica's hand for a second, and her breath caught in her chest. *Breathe*, she told herself.

"Now I see how you got in the middle of this thing." Tony shook his head.

"You in or out?" Sophie asked.

"I'm in," Tony said.

Jessica tried to concentrate on the conversation.

"We know the owners and they know us. Mom's at a meeting, so let's ask Dad about going in. Then we can call the owners and get permission if he thinks we need to."

Jessica thought it went well when they asked her uncle. There was just one catch. He was driving them over there, checking the place out first, then standing guard in the car. Tony called his parents about going, and they thought it was fine as long as Lucas Sandoval was going, too. Then Mr. Sandoval called the owners and got their permission to enter.

When they pulled up to it, Mr. Sandoval went inside, and the three of them sat in the car waiting, flashlights in hand. He turned on the lights inside the building and motioned them over.

As Sophie was stepping out of the car, she said. "Let's hurry. I just saw something move out there."

Tony shrugged. "Does it matter? I doubt anyone would follow us."

Jessica and Sophie looked at each other, and Sophie said, "I guess we forgot to tell him part of the story."

Tony looked over his shoulder. "You mean someone has been following you?"

"Uh-huh. Once he chased us all the way to the sheriff's office."

"Now I wonder if I should be glad I'm involved in this."
Sophie paused. "You can go home if you're chicken."

"No one's called me that since I was six. And he got a black eye for it. I'm going."

Sophie called to her dad, "We're going to walk around the building and see if there are any signs of a basement."

"I'm coming," he called back. He followed them as they studied the front, then walked around the corner of the block to the alley that went behind the building.

"There aren't any basement windows like on our building," Tony said.

"My mom's building doesn't have windows there. Let's go inside and try to find an entrance to a basement."

When they went around to the front again, Mr. Sandoval walked toward his car, saying, "I don't think you'll find a thing, but I'll be out here, just in case." He got inside, turned on the dome light and picked up a book.

Inside, the trio began their search in a back room that held a desk and phone.

"Our basement entrance is a flap in the floor. How do you get into your basement?" Sophie asked Tony.

"We use ours all the time for storage, so we have a regular door and stairs."

Sophie said, "Let's look for anything that seems strange. And remember, the FBI didn't notice it, so it won't be obvious."

Inside, Sophie stepped into the first empty room. Jessica and Tony continued down the hall. The three of them went from room to room, checking around and under furniture.

Soon Jessica could hear someone scuffling around in the room next to her. Then she heard Sophie say, "This is weird."

"What is?" Jessica came into the room with Sophie.

Sophie pointed at the wall. "This area is sun bleached and about the same size as the bookcase on the facing wall."

"That is weird. Hey, Tony," Jessica called.

He walked into the room. "Did you find something?"

"Sophie did. Someone must have moved this bookcase." Jessica pointed to the wall and told him about it. "You know, it's possible that they just needed it on another wall."

Tony said, "Let's see if anything's behind it."

The three of them pushed it to the side.

"A door!" Jessica exclaimed.

"Let's see what's behind this."

When Sophie reached for the doorknob, Jessica put her hand out to stop her. "Hey, maybe we should get your dad."

Sophie paused and looked like she was thinking about it. "Let's see if it's worth getting him. It might just be a closet." The door creaked as Sophie pulled it open. She said in a low voice, "There are stairs." Turning on her flashlight, she reached inside. "Let's see if there's a light switch."

When it flipped on, they could see that the stairs led to a dark basement.

"See anything down there?" Sophie whispered.

"Now who's chicken?" Tony laughed.

"I'm not chicken. I'm"—she paused—"cautious."

"That's a first." Jessica giggled.

Sophie glared at her, then grinned. "I think Dad might be angry if we don't get him right now."

Jessica said, "I think you are exactly right."

Sophie ran out of the room and came back with him.

His eyes opened wide when he saw the door and the stairs beyond. "You mean to tell me that you actually found something the FBI missed? Maybe we should call them."

"Dad, they haven't called us back, and we think Agent Dallas is missing and in there." Sophie pointed. "We have to rescue him."

He rolled his eyes. "Fine. Let's see if there's anything mysterious downstairs."

Sophie stepped through the doorway before anyone could stop her. Mr. Sandoval followed, then Tony and Jessica. Sophie stumbled slightly on the bottom step. "Watch that last step. It's taller than the others."

Mr. Sandoval and Tony came down the stairs fine, but Jessica took the last step flying, hit the concrete on her knees, and slid across the floor.

"Are you all right?" Tony raced to her side.

Her knees stung but her face felt hotter. She thought, *Just completely humiliated*, but said, "I'm okay." She felt stupid but liked it when Tony helped her to her feet.

He said, "This is a small and neat, empty basement. There isn't a single piece of junk and only a little bit of dust and a few cobwebs."

Sophie banged her hand on her fist. "This is frustrating. I thought we'd found a clue."

"But, Sophie," Jessica asked, "if there was nothing to hide, why was the bookcase moved?"

Tony walked around the room. "Look here. It's cobweb-free in this corner." He gestured to the rest of the basement. "*Only* in this corner."

"And there's a storage area with shelves there. It's kind of a bookcase, and a bookcase hid a door upstairs," Jessica added.

"Jessica, I doubt anyone would use the same ploy twice," Mr. Sandoval said.

"I'd be cleverer," Sophie agreed.

Tony put his head against the wall and tried to peer behind the bookcase. "I can't see anything." He and Mr. Sandoval pushed it to the side.

"Another door," Sophie whispered.

26

Daring Rescue

"Calling the sheriff might take too long. I think we should go in there and rescue Agent Dallas." Sophie crossed her arms and stood firmly in her place. They needed to do this.

"My dear cousin, we don't know if he's there. He might be having dinner at the resort right now. This place might be filled with bad guys. Or rats."

"I'm not afraid." Tony glared at Sophie. "I wouldn't want to find criminals or rats, but I think we should see what's in there."

Mr. Sandoval sighed. "I can't believe I'm agreeing with your reasoning, but let's go in." He shook his head. "What will your mother say, Sophie?"

As Tony slowly opened the door, Sophie crouched low and peered through the gap. She first saw a single lightbulb dangling from the ceiling in the middle of the room, giving off a small amount of light. Then, as the door swung wider, she could see a man sitting on the floor, tied, blindfolded, and gagged. A strange sound came from inside the room.

Sophie stood. "I was right. There's Agent Dallas."

"No, it's Mr. Merkle, the shoe salesman who came into the deli," Tony whispered beside her.

The other three looked at him.

Sophie smiled and nodded. "I get it. Being a shoe salesman was his cover story."

"Must be. Who goes first?" Tony gestured toward the room.

"I will." Sophie started through the door.

"Soph," Mr. Sandoval whispered, but she didn't stop.

When Sophie stepped into the room, she could see a woman sleeping on a cot in the corner, wrapped in a fur coat and wearing red high-heeled shoes. The strange sound she'd heard earlier was her snoring in a way that sounded like a chainsaw cutting through metal. Sophie turned back and whispered, "Get her," then pointed toward the woman.

She heard Jessica say, "Who?" Then, "Oh."

As Sophie crouched next to Agent Dallas, she saw her dad move to stand over the woman, ready to pin her down if she woke up. Jessica had pulled off her belt and was wrapping it around the woman's hands. When she tightened it, the woman awoke and kicked out at them until Tony sat on her legs.

"That will keep her still," he said.

Sophie untied Agent Dallas, then removed his gag. "Are you all right?" she asked as she started on the blindfold.

When the blindfold was removed, he blinked and rubbed his eyes. "I am now."

Mr. Sandoval helped Agent Dallas to his feet.

"Let's get her over to the sheriff's office," Agent Dallas

ordered and took a step toward the bound woman. Then he weakly slumped against Mr. Sandoval. "I'm weaker than I thought." Tony supported him from the other side as they made their way out of the basement.

Sophie and Jessica pulled the woman to her feet. She didn't fight them, so she must have sensed they had her outnumbered.

As they pushed her along behind the men, the woman said, "You nosy girls. Our plan was going well until you stuck your noses in this."

Maybe she'd spill the whole story if she thought they already knew about the crime. Sophie said, "That day at the Down Shoppe, we didn't believe you were French."

The woman glared at them. "I remembered just enough French from high school to throw you off."

"So it *was* her," Sophie said.

"Who's he?" The woman gestured with her head toward Tony.

"Never mind. How did you think you would get away with such a scheme?" Sophie asked.

Jessica looked puzzled. "What are—"

"Jessica, she knows we've figured it all out. We were smarter than they were."

"Ha! You kids don't know anything."

Sophie went through the clues one by one in her mind. Feathers, newspaper clippings, real estate contract . . . yes. "You tried to buy Mom and Dad's businesses to get us off your trail."

"They wouldn't sell, so I tried to scare you today so you'd leave town for a while—but you weren't home."

"You planned everything so you would have access to all the stores in Pine Hill," Jessica added.

Sophie stared at her cousin in amazement. Could she be onto something?

The woman turned to Jessica. "You do know! We were going to rob this town."

Sophie felt like a lightbulb had switched on. "You planned to steal and use the tunnels and connected basements to get everything out."

The woman sneered. "If you hadn't come along, we'd have cleaned this town out tomorrow night."

Jessica smiled at Sophie. Then they pulled the woman up the stairs, out the door, and down the street to the sheriff's office.

Sophie pushed open the door to the office. Sheriff Valeska slumped in her chair and sighed. "What now, girls? I'm almost ready to leave for the night."

When Sophie pulled the woman in behind her, the sheriff's mouth dropped open. And when a grimy and weak Agent Dallas followed, supported by Mr. Sandoval and Tony, she seemed frozen in her chair. Agent Dallas stumbled, almost pulling all three men to the ground. Sheriff Valeska jumped to her feet and pulled a chair over to the agent. "Here. Sit down."

"Please lock this woman up," he said in a shaky voice as he sat. "She and her husband surprised me one night in the dark, knocked me out, and kidnapped me."

Sheriff Valeska took the woman away. When she returned, she said, "That looked like the fur coat that the owner of Elegance Furs reported missing and assumed shoplifted.

Her red shoes must be the ones stolen from Simpson's."
She sat down and said, "Tell me what happened."

"These four just rescued me from the Down Shoppe's basement."

Sophie thought about telling him that it was really Hook, Line & Sinker but didn't think he'd care right now.

"There was a basement? The FBI didn't find one."

Agent Dallas sighed and leaned back in his chair. "I heard many footsteps over my head earlier, and thought I was about to be rescued. Then it got quiet." He sniffed the air. "That coffee sure smells good."

"I'll get it for you. I'm used to getting coffee." Tony walked over to the coffee maker.

The agent looked confused at Tony's statement. Sophie explained, "His family owns Donadio's Deli."

Agent Dallas smiled weakly. "I knew he seemed familiar. You guys make the best turkey on wheat that I've ever had."

Tony grinned. "My mother thanks you. Cream or sugar?" he asked.

"Two sugars." Agent Dallas ran his hand through his hair.

"How did you end up in that basement?" Sheriff Valeska asked.

"I sent my partner to follow Jessica and Sophie. Then I circled through the woods toward town. That's the last I remember until I woke in what felt like a basement, with my hands and feet tied, tape over my mouth, and a blindfold." The agent sighed in a way that almost sounded like a groan. "I have no idea how long I was there."

"It's Wednesday."

Agent Dallas leaned forward in his chair and rested his elbows on his thighs. "Four days. It seemed longer than that." Then he sat straight in his chair. "I need to call Agent Able."

Sheriff Valeska handed him the phone just as Tony gave him his cup of coffee. He looked at both and seemed too tired to figure out what to do, so Tony took the cup from him and set it on the desk.

"Thanks. I'm a little confused." He dialed the phone and hung up a few seconds later. "No answer. Have any of you seen Agent Able?"

Jessica shrugged. "We don't know what he looks like."

"He's tall and thin, brown hair, mustache, often wore dark pants and a tan jacket."

The girls looked at each other.

"He's the man who chased us."

"Chased you?" Agent Dallas took a sip of his coffee and closed his eyes. "I missed this." After another sip, he said, "Yes, it's coming back to me. I remember you said someone chased you."

Jessica said, "We assumed a bad guy chased us, but we felt fairly confident that the man wore a tan jacket and navy pants. It must have been Agent Able."

"I told him to follow you. He's very efficient, so if he thought you were in danger, he might have given chase when you ran." Agent Dallas rubbed his eyes. "Have you seen him since then?"

The girls looked at each other again, and Sophie answered, "No. But we don't really know what he looks like up close."

He turned toward Tony. "Able loved your family's chicken salad on rye. Has anyone ordered one lately?"

"I remember an order that we delivered to the resort this afternoon."

Agent Dallas sighed with obvious relief. "We were staying there. Maybe he's out searching for me and will be back later."

One thing still didn't make sense to Sophie. "We left messages for you, but no one returned them."

He looked at her oddly. "No one?"

Sophie answered. "No one."

"Strange." He nodded his head, obviously considering what they'd said as he took a long sip of his coffee.

"Can I give you a ride back to the resort?" Sheriff Valeska asked.

Agent Dallas nodded. "Yes. But I'm filthy. I'd love a ride to the *back door* of the resort."

Jessica giggled and held her nose.

He raised his eyebrows at her, then smiled. "I'd be offended if I had enough energy."

Mr. Sandoval stood and offered, "I'll get our car and bring it around here so we can give Agent Dallas a ride. You've got enough to do here, Mandy."

While they waited, Sophie asked, "What about the woman we brought in?" She pointed toward the back of the sheriff's office.

Agent Dallas and Sheriff Valeska looked surprised, as though they'd forgotten about her. The sheriff said, "We can hold her on the kidnapping charge. Tomorrow we'll sort everything else out."

"We'll be here first thing," Sophie said.

The sheriff said, "Stay home. We can handle it, girls."

Sophie raised one eyebrow. "I guess you don't want to know what she told us." Her dad had pulled his car in front of the building, so she started to walk out the door.

"Okay, be here about eight," Sheriff Valeska called after her.

"Hey, what about me?" Tony asked. A second later he said, "Never mind. My sister's gone tomorrow, so I have to be at the deli. But please let me know what happens."

They dropped off Agent Dallas, then Tony, and finally pulled into Sophie's driveway. Her father turned off the lights and opened his car door. "We're a lot later getting home than I'd expected. I hope your mother wasn't too concerned about us, Sophie. At least we know that Agent Dallas is back on the job."

As they started up the steps, Mrs. Sandoval stood in the doorway, waving her jacket. "Where have you been for so long? I've been out looking for you."

"Sorry," Mr. Sandoval said. "We rescued Agent Dallas." He hung his coat in the closet.

"You're kidding." She sat on the sofa.

"Nope. The kids were right about him. Girls, go get clean clothes on, and let's have some popcorn."

"Yes!" Sophie pulled her fist through the air. They ran into the bedroom, changed their clothes, and were back in minutes. A bowlful of popcorn already sat on the coffee table.

The girls told Mrs. Sandoval all about what had happened. As she listened, she popped the popcorn in her mouth, handful after handful, like she was at an exciting movie.

"Wow. Until this 'George' is caught, I'm keeping you girls with me at Great Finds."

"Can't do." Sophie grabbed a handful of the popcorn. "Tomorrow morning we have to go to the sheriff's office. They're going to interrogate the woman and said we could watch since we tricked her into telling the truth about the crime."

27

Sweet Solution

Mr. Sandoval dropped the girls off at 8 a.m. at the sheriff's office, then drove to a meeting with a client. Sophie noticed that Agent Dallas looked well rested. They sure trained FBI agents to recover quickly.

He greeted them when they walked in. "Nice to see you girls. Now that I've had a couple of meals and can think clearly, I have to thank you again. What you did still amazes me."

"You're welcome." Jessica blushed at the praise.

"And Agent Able is safe. He spent a lot of his time following you and searching for clues to my location. I found him in his room last night, eating the leftover half of his sandwich from the deli."

Sophie and Jessica laughed and sat down.

"Able chased you because he thought you were in trouble when you ran. He didn't know you'd only run because you'd seen him behind you." He sighed.

"Why didn't he call us back when we left messages?" Sophie asked.

Agent Dallas grimaced. "I'm embarrassed to say this after everything you've done, but he recognized your names and didn't think kids could help."

Sophie almost got mad, but then she remembered how much they *had* helped, and Agent Dallas did seem grateful.

"Let's see what my kidnapper has to say for herself." He nodded at Sheriff Valeska, and she went to the back for the prisoner.

When they returned, Jessica stared at the woman. "We didn't just see you at the Down Shoppe. You stood out wearing flowers on a dress and hat."

"After ugly prison clothes, I liked wearing things with flowers on them. I got to wear anything I wanted, including furs." The woman glared at them.

Agent Dallas leaned back comfortably in his chair. "Now you'll get what the law wants—a new prison sentence."

Sheriff Valeska turned to the girls. "Tell us what she said to you last night."

The woman jumped in. "Those girls have been trouble from the first day they knocked on the door to the Down Shoppe. We tried to buy the building the mother's business is in and even offered to buy the father's business to get them to leave town." She slowly grinned in a way that made Sophie shudder. "That antique shop is also right next to a fur store and on an alley where we could park a large truck."

Jessica explained. "They planned to use the tunnels to steal from every business in town."

"Tunnels? Steal?" Agent Dallas leaned forward, intent on her words.

"Sophie and I, uh, *found* connected basements and tunnels under Pine Hill. They planned to break into the businesses through the tunnels. We heard them talking. Her name's Eva."

Eva glared at them. "A man we met in prison told us about the basements and tunnels under Pine Hill. His grandfather helped build them. He also had old newspapers that said the town was loaded with money from tourists." She put her hands on her hips and chuckled. "Even before we got out of jail, we had a great idea. We could use stairs for access, and when there weren't any, we would cut away pieces in the floor above so that it would only take a few minutes to break through into the shops. Jewelry, furs, money, antiques. We would have gotten away with it all."

Sophie sat on the edge of the sheriff's desk. "So it wasn't all my fault that I fell through the floor. You made it break more easily."

Eva nodded. "We'd already taken care of the entrance under your mother's shop. You girls caused more problems for us after you fell through the floor and found that we'd stuck those stupid comforters of George's there. After he bungled them, we thought they might still turn out to be useful as a soft place to land if we were in the antique shop and needed a quick escape." She sneered and pointed at the girls. "They got the briefcase full of down, full of what was supposed to go into the window to make us look legit. When George went back the next day, the idiot couldn't find either of them."

"George who?"

"I shouldn't have told you anything." Eva crossed her arms and glared at them. "I'm not saying another word until I get a lawyer."

Sophie tried another question. "Did you think you could steal things as you went?"

Eva chuckled. "This coat and shoes were my prizes. George can unlock anything. Not another word." This time she stayed silent.

Sheriff Valeska signaled for a deputy to take her back to her cell.

Agent Dallas stood. "I guess that's it. They'd planned a big heist. I wonder what gave them all their crazy ideas."

"One of the pieces of newspaper we found had an article about the old Down Shoppe on one side and that article on the other about the amount of money visitors spend here each summer."

All of the clues were coming together. "Maybe when they came to town and Hook, Line & Sinker was closed, they decided to take it over and re-create the business they'd read about over and over again in those clippings—the Down Shoppe. That's why George had the down."

Jessica said, "They probably figured no one would remember it from before or try to find out what happened to the owners of the store that was supposed to be there." She smiled at Sophie. "They shouldn't have done that. Not in a small town."

Sophie said, "Exactly. Can you imagine if they'd cleaned out every shop in Pine Hill?" She rested her chin in her hands as she thought. "Whew, they must have planned to have a huge truck ready that night."

Agent Dallas shook his head. "You girls solved the whole thing. But until we find 'George,' stay out in the open."

"We know." Jessica sighed, obviously frustrated.

"We never get to be part of the action," Sophie muttered when the door to the sheriff's office closed behind her.

Jessica stopped in her tracks. "Are you kidding?"

Sophie laughed. "We did rescue an FBI agent."

"When no one else could find him. And captured a criminal."

While they walked up the street toward Great Finds, Jessica pointed at a man across the street. "That's . . . that's . . ."

Sophie studied him. "That's the man in the brown suit. George."

Jessica nodded and gulped.

"Let's turn around and tell the sheriff."

"Good idea. Hurry." Jessica pushed Sophie along the sidewalk. "Oh, no."

Sophie glanced around. "What?"

"He's coming this way. I think he's seen us. Run!"

Sophie and Jessica ran down the street.

"I've got an idea." Sophie panted between words. "Go ahead of me to Bananas and get two banana cream pies from Mrs. Bowman. I sure hope she has some."

She slowed down to give Jessica time to get there ahead of her. When Sophie ran into the bakery, Jessica set a pie in her hand. The man pushed through the door a second later. Sophie hit him in the face with her pie. Then Jessica splatted hers on top of that. He clawed at his face to pull off the creamy mess.

"Push him down," Sophie shouted and shoved at his back.

Mrs. Bowman shrieked when the man hit the floor.

Jessica sat on him. "We need to tie him up." She looked around frantically for something to use. "Hurry."

Sophie tried to pin down his arms. "Use your belt again."

Jessica looked down and nodded. She unfastened it and wrapped it around the man's wrists. He started bucking and fighting, kicking with his feet so hard that bits of pie flew off him and splattered onto them. "Tie his feet," Jessica shouted when he almost kicked her off.

When Sophie sat on his feet, Mrs. Bowman ran over with a roll of string.

"You tie his ankles," Jessica ordered.

The older woman looked timidly at the man's feet, then stepped forward and wrapped the string around them.

Sophie glanced over at the phone on the wall. "Now we'd better call the sheriff."

Just then Sheriff Valeska and a deputy rushed through the door.

Sophie looked up at them, confused.

Mrs. Bowman answered the silent question. "I called the sheriff, Sophie, after you hit him with the pies. I didn't know what was going on."

"Thank you. Sheriff, we think this is George." Sophie and Jessica stood.

"How do you kids know my name?" the startled man sputtered.

"Because we freed the FBI agent last night and captured Eva."

The sheriff and her deputy pulled the man to his feet and directed him through the open door. He muttered, "I hate bananas."

"Well—" Mrs. Bowman exclaimed. "How rude."

Going out the door, Sophie said to Jessica, "There isn't anything worse to her than someone who hates bananas."

"It's a good thing she had banana cream pies today. We owe her for them."

Sophie started laughing. "I just thought of something. I think you can say that we creamed him."

Read
The Treasure Key,
the next book in
the Crime-Solving
Cousins Mystery
series.

One More Puzzle

One question is left unanswered in the book. Mrs. Bowman, the owner of the bakery, is seen in front of the Down Shoppe and she's overheard talking about down. Jessica and Sophie are suspicious of her. Is she involved in "The Feather Chase"?

After you've read the book, solve the last piece of the mystery. Fill in the blanks. Then write the correct number of letter on the blank at the bottom.

The name of the bakery. $\underline{}\ \underline{}\ \underline{}\ \underline{}\ \underline{}\ \underline{}\ \underline{}$
$\qquad\qquad\qquad\quad\ \ 4\ \ 7\ \ 8\ \ 7\ \ 8\ \ 7\ \ 3$

They found the feathers in this. $\underline{}\ \underline{}\ \underline{}\ \underline{}\ \underline{}\ \underline{}\ \underline{}\ \underline{}\ \underline{}$
$\qquad\qquad\qquad\qquad\qquad\ \ 4\ \ 2\ \ 9\ \qquad\qquad\ 7\ \ 3$

Who found the suitcase first? $\underline{}\ \underline{}\ \underline{}\ \underline{}\ \underline{}\ \underline{}$
$\qquad\qquad\qquad\qquad\qquad\ 3\ \ 5\qquad\ \ 9$

Sophie lives in this town. $\underline{}\ \underline{}\ \underline{}\ \underline{}\ \underline{}\ \underline{}\ \underline{}$
$\qquad\qquad\qquad\qquad\ \ 9\ \ 8\qquad\qquad\ \ 13\ 13$

What was mixed with the feathers? $\underline{}\ \underline{}\ \underline{}\ \underline{}$
$\qquad\qquad\qquad\qquad\qquad\quad\ 5\ \ 6$

Sophie likes pineapple on her $\underline{}\ \underline{}\ \underline{}\ \underline{}\ \underline{}$.
$\qquad\qquad\qquad\qquad\ \ 3\ \ 12\ 8\qquad\ 7$

Sophie and Jessica solved a $\underline{}\ \underline{}\ \underline{}\ \underline{}\ \underline{}\ \underline{}$.
$\qquad\qquad\qquad\qquad\ 1\qquad 3\ 10\quad 2\ 14$

They saw these animals in the basement. $\underline{}\ \underline{}\ \underline{}\ \underline{}$
$\qquad\qquad\qquad\qquad\qquad\qquad\quad 2\ \ 7\ 10\ 3$

The sheriff took Sophie's $\underline{}\ \underline{}\ \underline{}\ \underline{}\ \underline{}\ \underline{}\ \underline{}\ \underline{}\ \underline{}$.
$\qquad\qquad\qquad\ \ 9\ \ 8\ 11\quad 2\quad\ 2\qquad 10\ 3$

$\overline{1}\ \overline{2}\ \overline{3}\quad \overline{4}\ \overline{5}\ \overline{6}\ \overline{1}\ \overline{7}\ \overline{8}\quad \overline{9}\ \overline{3}\quad \overline{8}\ \overline{5}\ \overline{10}\quad \overline{11}\ \overline{12}\ \overline{9}\ \overline{13}\ \overline{10}\ \overline{14}$

If you need help, find more clues and the answers at www.shannonlbrown.com.

About the Author

Shannon Brown loved reading mysteries as a kid. She still does, but now she's excited that she gets to write them too. When she isn't in the middle of a mystery, she likes to hike, shop, and bake. Originally from Alaska, she now lives in Tennessee with her professor husband. She enjoys writing at her desk with her calico cat Evie on her lap. To learn more about Shannon or about the Crime-Solving Cousins Mysteries, visit www.shannonlbrown.com.

CPSIA information can be obtained
at www.ICGtesting.com
Printed in the USA
BVHW081129031122
650948BV00005B/495